SO-BZI-858

This Book is Dedicated To My:

Family, Readers and Supporters. I LOVE you guys so much.
Please believe that!!

A Publisher's Note

Think of David vs. Goliath and yes the underdog won!! I've been in a vicious legal battle with Triple Crown Publications and Vickie Stringer for almost 2 years now. This fight has been draining on me and my family but I refused to lie down and let the wrong that had been done to me, defeat me! My mother once told me, "You have not because you ask not." I asked for it and it was delivered. I feel as if I stood up and fought for all the little people who are cheated, manipulated and done dirty in a cutthroat business. With faith and determination we shall continue to rise to the top! I feel blessed that the entire Bitch Series is under its rightful home, A King Production. I put my heart and soul into these books for my fans and now I know when I leave this earth my family can reap the rewards of my work. Soon I will upload video blogs to my website and Facebook page detailing my long legal journey and how I came to get the rights back to my books. Many said it couldn't be done but never underestimate one of God's children!! You know I had to share this because I LOVE my readers so much and I hope that I can prevent many of you from making some of the same mistakes I did. So please keep hope alive. If anybody in your life is doing you wrong, rebel and stand up for your rights. You will prevail!!

Hugs and Kisses from Your Literary Sweetheart!!

Joy Deja King

Acknowledgments

Special Thanks To...

Linda Williams; You said it would happen and you were right! You always believed in me and stayed true and loyal. That means everything to me.

Jonesy; You were the first radio personality that embraced my books! You set Bitch on fire in New York and I will forever love you for that!! Now you can set it back on fire under A King Production!! Kisses to you!

Tracy Taylor; Girl, you stay grindin' for the cause and be cute doing it!

Ann Hopson; I see you girl..."You're so Pretty."☺

Tazzy; I still adore you because I can always count on you being you!!
Keith Saunders; You're my dude!! Enough said...

Book Bullies; I see you making ish happen in 2010!!

Tureko "Virgo" Straughter, Renee Tolson, Jeanni Dixon, Ms KiKi, Andrea Denise, Sunshine716, Ms. (Nichelle) Mona Lisa, Lady Scorpio, Travis Williams, Brittney, Donell Adams, Myra Green, Leona Romich, Sexy Xanyell. To vendors and distributors like African World Books, Teddy Okafor, Black & Nobel, DaBook Joint, The Cartel, LaQuita Adams, DCBookman, Tiah, Vanessa and Glenn Ledbetter, Junior Job, Anjekee Books, Andy Carter, Urban Xclusive DVD & Bookstore, Future Endeavors. Also, to Yvette George, Velva White, Carla Stotts and the rest of Diva's of Memphis, Devin Steel, Big Sue, Thaddeus Mathews, Sherita Nunn, James Davis, Marcus & Wayne Moody, Trista Russell, Don Diva and Dolly Lopez…thank you all for your support!!

Special, special thanks to Cover 2 Cover Book Club; Christian Davis, Angela Slater, Pamela Rice, Ahmita Blanks, Melony Blanks, Marcia Harvey, Melinda Woodson, Tonnetta Smith, Tiffany Neal, Miisha Fleming, Tamika Rice and Bar. I so enjoyed our book chats for "Hooker to Housewife" and "Superstar". All of you ladies are wonderful!!

A KING PRODUCTION

Bitch

The Beginning...

Joy Deja King

Bitch

The Beginning...

Can't Knock the Hustle

Coming from nothing and having nothing are two different things. Yeah, I came from nothing, but I was determined to have it all. And how couldn't I?

I exploded into this world when "Hood Rich" wasn't an afterthought, but the only thought. You turn on the television and every nigga is iced out with an exotic whip sitting on 24inch rims, surrounded by a bitch in a g-string, a weave down to her ass, poppin' that booty. So the chicks on the videos were dropping it like it's hot for the rappers and singers while the bitches around my way were dropping it for our own superstars. Dealing with a street nigga on say the Alpo status a legendary drug kingpin was like being Beyoncé herself on Jigga Man's arm.

A bitch like me was thirsty for that. I'd been on some type of hustle since I was in Pampers.

I grew up in the grimiest Brooklyn projects during the '90s. It was worse than being in prison because you knew there was something better out there; you just didn't know how to get it. You never saw green grass or flowers blooming. Instead of looking up to teachers, lawyers or doctors, you worshipped the local drug dealers who hustled to survive and escape their existence. Even as a little girl, I knew I wanted more out of life. Somehow hustling was in my blood.

First, I hustled for my moms' attention because she was too busy turning tricks to pay me any mind. I never knew who my daddy was, so while my moms was fucking in her bedroom, I would wait outside the door with my legs crossed, holding my favorite teddy bear in one arm as I sucked my thumb. When the tricks would come out, I would look at them with puppy-dog eyes and ask, "Are you my daddy?" The question would freak them out so badly they'd toss me a few dollars so I would shut the fuck up.

One day when I was five, my mother was looking for something in my drawers, she came across a bunch of fives and tens and some twenties. The total was five hundred and some change. Of course, she wanted to know where all the money came from. When I told her that the money came from her business clients (that's what my moms called them), she lit up. She tossed me up in the air and said, "Baby, you my good luck charm. I knew one day you'd make me some money."

On that rare occasion she showed me mad love. As young as I was, I equated my mother's newfound interest in me with love. From that moment on, I learned how to hustle for my moms' attention – that is, by providing her with money.

Where I grew up, everyone hated "The Man," so they wouldn't report shit, even child abuse or neglect. When I was really young, my neighbors helped look out for me, when necessary. One neighbor, Mr. Duncan, used to baby-sit me while my mother "Worked." In the projects, we all minded our own business and had the same code of silence that the police have among themselves – we didn't snitch on each other.

Somehow, my moms' customers never messed with or even fondled me. I think it's because people say I got these funny looking eyes. Even when I was little I had an attitude that said, "Don't fuck wit' me."

By the time I was fifteen with all the tricks my moms pulled, we were still dead ass broke, living in the Brooklyn projects. She couldn't save a dime because with hooking comes drugging and my moms stayed high. I guess that's all you can do to escape the nightmare of having all types of nasty, greasy fat motherfuckers pounding your back out every damn day. The characters that I saw coming in and out of our apartment were enough to make me want to sew up my pussy so nobody could get between my legs.

One day when I came home from school, I found my moms sprawled out on the couch with a half empty bottle of whiskey in one hand, as she tried to toke her last pull off a roach in the other hand. Her once long, wavy sandy hair was now thin and straggly. The curves that once made every hood chick roll their eyes in envy were just a bag of bones. You wouldn't even recognize the one time ghetto queen unless you looked into the green eyes she inherited from her mulatto father.

Without a word, I gave the living room a lick and a promise. I emptied several full ashtrays, picked up the dirty glasses scattered about the floor and wiped off the cocktail table. Out of the corner of my eye, I watched my moms sit up and stare at me for a long five minutes. She had the strangest look on her face.

Finally she spoke up. "Precious, you sure are growing up to be a pretty girl." Although we were in each other's face on an everyday basis, it was as if this were the first time my mother had seen me in many years. I didn't know

3

how to respond so I kept cleaning up. "Didn't you hear what yo' mama said?"

"Yes, I heard you."

"Well you betta say thank you."

"Thank you, Mama."

"You welcome, baby."

As I continued to clean I couldn't help but feel uncomfortable with the glare my moms was giving me. It was the same look she'd get when she was about to get her hands on some prime dope.

"Baby, you know that your mother is getting up there in age. I can't put it down like I used to."

I looked my moms directly in the eye, but I said nothing. I was thinking to myself, *What the fuck that got to do wit' me"*

"So, baby, I was thinking maybe you need to start helping me out a little more."

"Help out more how, I basically give you my whole paycheck?" I didn't understand what the fuck she was talking about. I barely went to school because I had what was supposed to be a part time job at a car detailing shop.

Damn near every cent I made, I used to pay bills and maintain my appearance. I couldn't afford to rock all the brand name hot shit, but because I had style, I was able to throw a few cheap pieces together to make it look real official. Luckily I inherited my moms' beauty and body so I could just about make a potato sack look sexy.

"Baby, that little job you got ain't bringing home no money. It's just enough to maintain. I'm talking about getting a real job."

"Mama, I'm only fifteen. It's only so many jobs I can get and so much money I can make. Boogie not even suppose to give me all the hours he have me doing at the shop. That's why he pays me under the table."

"Precious, as pretty as you are you can be making thousands of dollars."

"Doing what? What job you know is going to pay a fifteen-year-old high school student thousands of dollars?"

"The oldest profession in the book-sex," my moms said as if she was asking me to do something as innocent as baking cookies for a living.

"You 'un lost your damn mind. What you tryn' to be now - my pimp?"

"You betta watch yo' mouth, little girl. I'm yo' mama. Don't forget that."

"Don't you forget it. You must have if you asking me to sell my ass so I can take care of you."

"Not me - us. Shit, I took care of yo' ass for the last fifteen years. Breaking my back and wearing out my pussy to provide us with a good life."

"This is what you call a good life?" I said as I looked around the small, broke down, two bedroom apartment. The hardwood floors were cracking, the walls had holes and the windows didn't even lock. It was nothing to catch a few roaches holding court in the kitchen and living room, or a couple of rats making a dash across the floor.

My moms stood up and started fixing her unruly hair, patting down her multicolored flannel pajamas and twisting her mouth in that 'how dare you' position as if she were an upstanding citizen who was being disrespected in her own home.

"You listen here," she began as she pointed her bony finger with its gnawed down nail. "A lot of these children around here don't even have a place to stay. It might not be much but it's mine."

That, too, was a lie. My moms didn't even own this raggedy-ass apartment; she rented it. But I didn't feel like reminding her of that because I wanted this going-nowhere conversation to be over.

"I hear you, Ma, but I don't know what to tell you. I'm not following in your footsteps by selling my pussy to some low down niggas for money."

"Well then you betta start looking for some place to live, 'cause I can't take care of the both of us."

"You tryna tell me you would put me out on the streets?"

"You ain't leaving me a choice, Precious. If you can't bring home some extra money, then I'll have to rent out your bedroom to pay the bills."

"Who is gon' pay you for that piece of shit of a room?"

"Listen, I ain't 'bout to sit up here and argue wit' you. Either you start bringing home some more money or find another place to live. It's up to you. But if you don't give me a thousand dollars by the first of the month, I need you out by the second."

With that my moms' skeletal body disappeared into her dungeon of a bedroom. She was practically sentencing me to the homeless shelter. There was no way I could give her a thousand dollars a month unless I worked twenty-four hours a day, seven days a week at the detail shop. But what made this so fucked up was that my moms basically wanted me to pay for her out-of-control drug habit. This wasn't even about the bills because our Section 8 rent and other bills totaled no more than four hundred dollars a month. Because the street life had beaten down my moms, she was beating me over the head with bullshit.

With my moms giving me no way out, I began my own hustle. I decided to get the money by selling my ass, but I was going to pick and choose who was able to play between my legs. My job at the car detailing shop came in handy. Nothing but top-of-the-line hustlers parlayed through, but before, I never gave them the time of day. They were always trying to holla at a sistah, but the shade I gave them was thick.

Boogie, my boss, appreciated that. He was an older dude who took his illegal drug money and opened up his shop. He was in his forties, donned a baldhead and wore two basketball sized diamond studs in each ear. He wore sweat suits and a new fresh pair of sneakers everyday. He could afford any type of car he wanted, but he remained loyal to Cadillac Devilles. He had three: one in red, white and black.

"Boogie, who that nigga in the drop-top Beamer?" I asked when some dude I'd never seen before pulled up.

"Oh that's Azar. He moved here from Philly, why you ask?"

"I ain't neva seen him 'round here before, and I wanted to know who he was."

"Is that all, Precious?" Boogie asked, knowing it was more than that.

"Actually, to keep it real wit' you Boogie I'm looking for a man."

"What?" Boogie stopped dead in his tracks. "Looking for a man? One of the reasons I digged you so much, Precious, was because you wasn't fucking with none of these hustlers that came through here. Why the sudden change?"

"I'm not gonna get into all that Boogie, but I will tell you I really don't have a choice. I need money and fucking wit' a fo-sho nigga seems to be the only way to get it."

"Precious, you are much too young to have those types of worries. I could always give you a raise."

"Boogie, unless that raise is a few thousand dollars then it ain't gonna do me no good." Shit, I figured if I had to give my moms a thousand dollars a month, I might as well make a few for me. If I had to sell my ass, then I might as well get top dollar.

"I don't know what you need all that money for, Precious, but if you looking to fuck with a baller, then let me school you on a few things. For one, get your fuck game right."

"What you mean by that?"

"I mean if you want one of these niggas out here to spend some serious paper on you, you gotta learn to sex them real good. You know you're a beautiful girl, so attracting a big timer's attention is the easy part. But to have a nigga willing to spend the way you want, your head and pussy game have to be on point. Just giving you something to think about."

I watched as Boogie went outside to talk to a few guys that just pulled up in G5's. I was still thinking about the advice he gave me. Boogie was right, if I wanted to really land a hustler and keep him, I had to get my fuck game in order. The funny thing was from watching my moms selling her ass all my life, it turned me off from sex. I was probably the last virgin in my hood. I definitely needed a lot of work, and I needed to find someone that I could practice on before I actually went out there and tried to find my baller.

After work I came home and my moms was lying in her regular spot on the dingy couch. She was so bad off that she would've had to pay a nigga to fuck her. I hated to see my moms so broken down. One thing I promised myself was that no matter what, I would never let myself go out like that. I would play niggas; they would never play me.

Sex You Up

Since time wasn't on my side, I only had a week to scope out all the dudes that were coming in and out the detailing shop. I was carefully seeking out my victim. He had to be cute, paid and, hopefully, willing to spend his money freely. In two more weeks it was going to be the first and my moms was still threatening to throw me the fuck out.

I had narrowed down my search to three dudes. The nigga Azar, was actually my first choice, because not only did he have the drop-top beamer, but he also came through in a Range and a big body Benz. He was a fine ma'fuckah, too. He put me in the mind of Allen Iverson, with the corn-rows and all. But Boogie forewarned me that the nigga was gangsta. You couldn't half-ass him. He wasn't just giving his money to any ol' random bitch. Yo' shit had to be tight.

Since I still hadn't learned how to fuck, I was a little skeptical about trying my hand with him. The other two dudes were some come up type niggas. They were always trying to kick it with me. They would hit me off with a hundred dollar tip when they paid. I knew them dudes would lace me with some real paper if I gave them some.

Plus they were only aight' in the looks department. They would pay me just so they could sport a dime piece. They were the easy marks, but I wanted Azar. Something about him made my pussy wet.

On a rare day of going to school I peeped my corny-ass neighbor Jamal. He was a real straight-laced type dude. He was a rare guy in the neighborhood who had a mother and father in his home. They were a hard working couple, but due to their lack of education, they were barely getting by.

Jamal was supposed to be their savior. See, Jamal was a certified genius. He was only in ninth grade but taking twelfth grade classes. There was no doubt he would get a full scholarship to any college of his choosing. All the top prep schools around the country wanted him to attend their school, but Jamal's parents refused to let him leave home.

They felt he was too young and would get brainwashed in the white man's world. So he just took all advanced classes in preparation for his college departure.

"What's up, Jamal?" I walked up beside him. His eyes damn near popped out of his thick-rimmed bifocals. Which didn't surprise me, because we had been living next to one another our entire lives and I never spoke more than two words to him besides, "Nigga move"?

"Precious." He paused for a minute, looking at me, not sure if he heard me correctly.

"Yeah, what's up, Jamal?" I asked in a sweet voice. "How you doing?"

"I'm doing okay. Just on my way home to study for an exam I have in a couple of days." I couldn't front, the dedication that dude had for his books was crazy. I had to admit I somewhat admired the ghetto nerd.

"That's cool. I was wondering if maybe we could study together. I've been working so hard at my part-time job that

I fell behind on a lot of work. I was hoping you could help me catch up. I know how smart you are."

By this time Jamal and I had stopped at the top of the stairs of our high school. He was the first to notice some students stopping and staring at our odd pairing. But I didn't give a damn. I needed this nigga so fuck what they thought.

"Precious, you want to study with me? But you don't even like me."

"Jamal, that's not true. I just always got so much to deal with." Everybody in the building and surrounding parts knew my moms was a crack whore. His parents would even come over sometimes complaining about hearing the bed banging up against their wall when my moms was servicing her clients. By the way Jamal was looking at me, I could tell he felt sorry for me. I don't normally like pity but whatever would accomplish what I needed to get done.

"OK. When do you want to study?" I knew Jamal was looking forward to helping me out, especially since he had a crush on me since he was eight years old.

"How about today?" I knew that seemed sudden, but time wasn't on my side.

"I don't know, Precious. I really need to study for my exam, how about Wednesday? By then I would've taken the test."

"Jamal, you know you'll ace that exam with your eyes closed. I really need you today." I could see that he was debating it in his mind so to warm him up I stroked his hand and said, "Please, Jamal, you do want me to pass." With that we headed home.

I knew Jamal's parents both worked two jobs and didn't get home until after nine. For the first hour we worked on English and Math. I was trying to pay attention and seem interested in what Jamal was teaching, but my mind was on something else. Finally I had to get down to the nitty gritty of what I needed him for. "Jamal, have you ever had sex before?"

"Excuse me?" Jamal belted out, looking obviously shocked by my question.

"You heard me. Has your little thing ever gotten wet off some pussy juices?" I knew my line of questions was making Jamal uncomfortable, but I had to get right to it.

"Precious, we're supposed to be studying, not talking about sex."

"I know, Jamal, but there's a reason for this. See, I'm a virgin." I could see Jamal eyeing me sideways as if I was lying. With my mother being a known whore and all, I'm sure I was the last person he expected to be a virgin.

I continued, "I'm interested in dating this guy, but see he is used to experienced women. If I tried to get with him and he knew I was a virgin, he would laugh at me like I was some little girl. I need to be able to hold my own when we get down to it."

"That's interesting, Precious, but how do I fit in with any of that?"

"I want to practice learning how to fuck on you." As soon as the words left my lips, Jamal's skinny ass fell off his chair and hit the hardwood floor. He patted his hands on the floor looking for the bifocals that flew off his face. It was obvious he was damn near blind without them so I went to assist him with his search. I knelt down and handed him his glasses and for the first time got a good look at Jamal. He wasn't bad looking; almost cute. He had full, thick eyebrows that highlighted his light reddish skin. His profound jaw line gave him an almost model look.

"Here you go, Jamal," I said as I put his glasses back on.

"Thanks, Precious," Jamal said as he brushed himself off and stood up extra straight, trying to pretend he wasn't embarrassed by his fall. "Where were we?" Jamal grabbed my English book, diverting his attention from the proposition I just made him.

"We were talking about us, Jamal. Why won't you let me sex you up? I'm pretty sure you'll enjoy it."

"Sex me up? Why me? Precious, you're the prettiest girl in our school, probably the prettiest girl I've ever seen. Any guy would love to be your first," he said in a way that echoed his confusion as to why I was interested in having sex with him.

"Listen, Jamal. Honestly, for some reason I feel I can trust you. I don't believe you'll run around telling everybody we fucked. You know how these clown-ass niggas out here are. They'd have a field day letting the whole hood know they popped my cherry. It's also very convenient because we live right next door to one another. Come on, Jamal. It'll be fun."

I tapped my foot as Jamal stood there thinking about who knows what-I had no idea. Any other boy in his position would give their right arm to have sex with me but he probably felt some kinda way. He probably figured he would remain a virgin until he was at least twenty-one and his first time would be with his wife. But if he was as smart with the ladies as he was with the books, he would jump at the once in a life time opportunity. How many boys were actually able to have sex with their first crush?

"OK, I'll do it." Jamal was quiet for a moment. "When do you want to get started?" Jamal questioned, probably hoping I would say in about a week. That would then give him time to watch some porno's that I'm sure his father had stashed somewhere, and practice his own moves. I know he secretly hoped that maybe this would turn into more than an experiment for me, and he could become my boyfriend.

"Today," I said as I began unbuttoning my jeans and pulling off my sweater. Before Jamal knew it, I was standing in front of him with just my bra and panties on. It was obvious the only woman he had seen in person with her bra and panties on was his mother and she definitely didn't look like me. Jamal's dick instantly perked up as he studied my smooth, unblemished skin. I grabbed the condom that was in my jean pocket and handed it to Jamal.

"We definitely not tryn' to make no babies up in here." By being so aggressive, I knew Jamal doubted my virginity story.

"Where do you want to do the deed at?"

"A bed would be nice," I said, wanting to get started. See, to me this was a job, a potential well-paying one. Jamal led me to his cramped bedroom full of scientific posters and what looked to be chemistry projects. He had to knock a pile of books off the center of his bed so we could get busy.

After Jamal just stood staring at me for five minutes, I realized I would have to lead the way. He was totally petrified, but it didn't matter because I planned on doing all the work anyway. After stripping him down to his underwear, I could see his dick trying to escape his boxer shorts. I was surprised that he was working with a nice-sized tool. I began reaching for his boxers, but he lightly pushed my hand away like he was scared.

"Come on, Jamal. We almost there. Ain't no reason for you to be afraid." He finally lay down on the bed, after he took off his underwear. I stepped out of my bra and panties and decided to ride him like a horse jockey.

I heard that if you want to have control over a man you need to ride him. I definitely wanted to control Azar, so my pony game had to be tight. I ripped open the condom package and slid it on Jamal's dick. I could feel his body shaking due his nervousness. It was a damn shame that the blind was leading the blind, but I had no doubt we would both be pros before long.

I lifted my ass on top and took the tip of Jamal's dick and slowly let it play with the lips of my pussy. Then as I started getting wet, I led it to the center of my clit. Jamal was now making low moans as I let the head go in a little deeper. I wanted to take my time because, shit, I was a virgin and I wanted to minimize the pain as much as possible. I then let another three inches slide inside of me and I let out a slight scream as he hit that spot.

Once I got over that hump, the next couple of inches weren't as bad and it started feeling good. It was feeling good to Jamal too, because his once low moans were reaching a much louder pitch. After about five minutes my wide hips began rocking in a seductive pace. I seemed like a natural. Before long I found myself turning around on his manhood and riding him from the back. Right when I was really getting into the groove, Jamal let out a loud "Ahhhh-hhh," as he bust a nut.

When I got up, Jamal took off his condom and noticed the slight traces of blood. He looked at me with a big grin and said, "You really were a virgin."

For the next week, everyday after school Jamal and I got our sex on. As I predicted, we became pros. We even performed oral sex on one another and he told me just how to suck it so I would have him cumming within minutes.

With only a week left before the first of the month, it was time to see if all my practice had paid off. With some money I had saved, I went and purchased a sexy Baby Phat outfit to wear to work. Although a bitch needed to hold on to her last dollar, I thought of this as an investment. Tomorrow I planned on landing Azar. I knew he had scheduled an afternoon full service detailing job, and I planned to look so damn good he would have no choice but to holla!

Irresistible Chick

I woke up early the next morning to put in extra time for my appearance. The Baby Phat one-piece jean jumpsuit I was rockin' was hot. I purchased some Steve Madden heels to set it off. I usually wore my hair in a long braid, but the night before, I put in a deep conditioner so my natural waves would hang smooth and free. I dapped on some clear lip gloss to give that just-gave-a-blowjob look.

When I stepped out my bedroom, to my disappointment, my moms was up earlier than usually. Her eyes bulged when she got a whiff of me. "Precious Cummings, where you going looking like dat?" she barked, holding on to her glass of whiskey. My moms couldn't get over how beautiful I looked. I was always pretty, but this was something else.

"Work."

"Work, looking like dat? Um, well, that outfit you got on looks awfully expensive. I hope you ain't playing wit' my paper."

"Ma, you'll have your money by the first. Now excuse me, I have a job to go to unlike some people." I slammed the door and headed for work before I fucked around and slapped the shit out of my moms.

When I got to work I only saw Boogie's car parked out front. I did come a little early because I didn't want to be stuck in the house with my drunken mother. Boogie was behind the cash register getting things in order before business officially started. "What's up, Boogie," I said as he counted some money. He nodded his head, acknowledging me but keeping his eyes on the money, not wanting to lose his count.

As I sat my belongings down the next thing I heard was, "Oh shit, what the fuck happened to you?"

"What you mean?" I asked, fully aware that he was speaking about my transformation. I usually came to work in jeans or sweats. So with my hair out and the form-fitting attire, I knew Boogie was in shock.

"Damn, baby, you is fine. I'm not trying to hit on you, because you are much too young for my blood, but baby, you are going to make somebody a lucky man."

"Why, thank you, Boogie. That is my hope." I tried to sound all proper.

"Who knew you had all that going on?" he added, shaking his head in disbelief.

For the next three hours all I did was turn down dudes offering me they number.

All they kept asking was, "Who's the new girl?" No one could believe that I was the same person.

They always thought I was pretty in a young girl way, but now I was looking like a woman. That shit was blowing their minds. Honestly, though, I didn't care what all the other dudes thought about me. I was only interested in impressing one person and that was Azar.

I was chewing my gum and blowing bubbles, dying for him to pull up. When the clock hit two o'clock, Azar pulled up in his brand new 2002 white CL600. I visualized myself flossing in the passenger seat next to him. We would be the

King and Queen of the streets.

Keeping to his normal routine, he sat outside and kicked it with the other fellas until his car was done. When he came inside, the first thing he asked was, "Where's the usual girl at?" In the few times he had been in here, I'd never heard his voice. He would hand me two bills and head out. The first couple of times when I tried to give him back his change, he would simply put his hand up, letting me know to keep it. He had a slick, sexy voice that complimented his look.

"It's me, I'm the same girl."

He studied me hard; trying to see what was different about me.

"I decided to let my hair down - that's all."

"My fault. I need to start paying better attention to what's right in front of my eyes."

"Don't worry about it," I said with a slight smile. *This nigga even lick his lips in the same sexy way Allen Iverson do after he completes a sentence,* I thought.

"Nah, I'd rather worry. To think all this time a pretty piece like you was right in front of me. That's a problem. We have to play catch up, "'cause you a real beauty."

"Thank you." Azar was making me blush. Mad niggas had told me I was beautiful before but not a dude on Azar's level. It was like if I were walking down the street and Bobby Valentino stepped to me and asked me to Slow Down.

"What's your name anyway?"

"Precious."

"That's sexy, just like you. How 'bout we go and catch a movie and dinner, Precious? Say tonight, if you not busy."

"I'd like that."

"Cool. What time you get off work."

"Seven."

"Alright. I'll be here then." When Azar exited, I wanted to jump up and down. I couldn't believe that, just like that, this dude was checking for me. Half of the work was done, now I needed to get him to give up some paper. Exactly how to get him to do that was something I felt needed to be discussed with Boogie. He was a playa. He would know what a playa does.

It was a quarter to seven when the last customer left and I finally had some alone time with Boogie. "Boogie, can I speak to you for a minute?"

"Yeah, what's up?"

"Boogie, Azar asked me out and he's picking me up from work today. He'll be here in fifteen minutes, so I don't have long to get your advice about something."

"I knew you had your eyes on that boy. So what you need my advice about?"

"How can I get Azar to spend his money on me?" I asked straight up. I knew I could be honest with Boogie like that. He believed women should come off, especially if she was fucking.

"I'm glad you asked me that, little lady. With this new look you have going on; men are going to be coming at you from all directions. It's important that if you want to get in this game, you play it correctly so you can get all you're worth. I personally think you're worth a lot. You're what I would call the top of the line, Precious. Hell, if you were ten years older I would make you mine. With that said, when you dealing with these hustlers on the street, you have to ask for what you want."

"Ask? Isn't that a little rude?"

"It's not what you ask; it's how you ask it. The same way a man is going to ask to get between your legs, the same way you ask him for whatever you want. Understand something, Precious. You're prime pussy. You can deal with any of these niggas out here. Starting with Azar is a good look. He's big time and low key with his shit. But after whatever you have going on with him is over, you can only fuck with niggas that are equal or above him. That's how you keep your stock up. That's how a lot of women pull themselves down. They start letting any ole type of piece of shit run up in them. No one is going to want to invest in that."

After Boogie said his last sentence, I saw Azar pull up. He arrived at seven o'clock on the dot. I grabbed my purse and said, "Thanks, Boogie," as I kissed him goodbye.

When I sat in Azar's car, I was in awe. I had never sat in a Benz before. Even though I worked in a detailing shop and flashy cars were coming in all the time, Boogie never let me leave from behind the cashier desk. He stressed he needed my presence up front at all times. My ass melted in the seat. It was the softest leather I had ever felt in my life. Azar's Benz was a custom white-on-white and his copper-toned complexion just glistened behind the wheel. Azar headed over the Brooklyn Bridge to the city. I rarely ever went to the city. It was like another world to me.

That night was crazy for me. Azar was the first date I had ever been on, and he came correct. After the movie he took me to some fancy restaurant, and I even had a drink. Nobody even bother to card me. I didn't want the night to end. When Azar pulled up to my apartment building I was surprised that he hadn't tried to make a move on me. When I was about to get out the car, he grabbed my arm. "I want to see you tomorrow."

"I'd like that."

"Good. What would you like to do?" I thought about what he asked for a second and decided to try my hand.

"I would love if you took me shopping. I want to look good for you." There was complete silence, and I wasn't sure if Azar was going to push me out his whip and speed off, offended by my suggestion. To my surprise he wasn't.

"I want you to look good for me, too. What time do you get off work tomorrow? I'll pick you up?"

"Actually, I have to go to school," I said wondering if he would start questioning my age."

"No problem, I'll pick you up from there."

"I'm in high school, Azar," I admitted, knowing he would eventually find out anyway.

"I figured that. Give me the time and address. I'll be there." After giving Azar the information he kissed me on the cheek and drove off. I was stunned at how cool he was. Although I knew Azar was only nineteen, I wasn't sure how he was going to take dealing with a fifteen year old.

When I opened the door to the apartment, some funky looking nigga was stumbling out. I looked him up and down and my moms said from the couch, "Oh, he was just look-ing at your bedroom. He's a potential tenant."

"That won't be necessary, you'll get your damn money," I said, slamming the door on the bum. I then walked to my room and slammed the door again.

The next day after school I rushed to get outside to meet Azar. I was looking forward to going shopping. When I reached the entrance to the school I was startled when Jamal approached me. I hadn't seen him in a couple of days.

"Where have you been, Precious? You haven't come over to study lately."

"I know, Jamal. Our studying is over. I learned everything I needed to."

"So just like that it's over?"

"Jamal, it never started. I told you from jump that I needed your help to prepare me for this boy I was interested in. Well, now he's interested so we done."

"Precious, wait," Jamal said as he grabbed my arm.

"Nigga, you betta get the fuck off me. Who you think you grabbing on?" I was burning a hole through Jamal. He was out of line putting his hands on me.

"Precious, I'm sorry. I didn't mean to grab your arm. I guess I miss you."

"Miss me? Jamal, we ain't in no relationship. It is what it is. We both got something out of it; now it's time to let it go. I'll see you around."

When I walked off, I knew Jamal was watching my every step. He must of felt some kinda way when he saw me get in the car with Azar. But that wasn't my problem. He knew there were no strings attached. It wasn't my fault if he caught feelings.

Once again Azar headed towards the bridge when I got in the car with him. "You really love the city don't you?"

"You said you wanted to go shopping. I'm taking you to the official stores so I can lace you right." I looked at Azar in shock. Never did I think we would go shopping in the city. I figured he would take me to Macy's at Kings Plaza, and I was excited about that. So when we pulled up to Saks 5th Avenue, my jaw dropped. Me and my girlfriend Inga used to talk about what it would be like to shop in a store like this. Never did I believe the day would actually come that it could.

"Damn, Azar, I ain't neva been in Saks before."

"That's why I'm glad you made the suggestion I take you shopping. If you gonna hang wit' me, yo' shit need to be tight. Your style is a reflection of me. The chick in my passenger seat gotta be on point."

That was hot. That must have meant Azar was planning on keeping me around for a minute. I smiled at the thought.

For the next week, Azar and I spent all our free time together. He would pick me up from school or from my job. Then we would either go out to eat, to the movies or just kick it at his crib. We still hadn't fucked, but Azar didn't seem to be stressing it. Before I knew it the first of the month had rolled around and I didn't have a dollar to my name. When Azar took me shopping, I swear he dropped three G's on me like it was nothing. But he still hadn't put cash money in my hands. It was true I hadn't asked for any, but still he never offered. After spending the day together, I knew I couldn't roll up in my moms' crib without her money. My hands were sweaty as I built up the nerve to ask Azar for the grand. I had to admit that we both seemed to be feeling each other, but I still didn't know just how cool we were. I kept thinking about what Boogie said. It's not what you ask, it's how you ask.

"Azar, I need you to do me a huge favor."

"What is it, Ma?"

"I know you took me on that fly-ass shopping spree, but I'm in a bit of a bind. My moms is stressing me to help her with her bills. I'm dead-ass broke and I was wondering if you could help me out." I held my head down the whole time I asked because I didn't want to see the look in his eyes. For all I knew, he could say to himself that this straight gold-diggin' bitch ain't getting a dime from me.

"How much you need?" he asked calmly.

"A thousand," I said, still looking down.

He pulled out a wad of cash and started counting out hundreds. He handed me the money and said, "Don't ever be afraid to ask me for nothing. As long as you're dealing wit' me, we cool. I got you."

Walking up the stairs to my apartment building, I counted the money Azar gave me and realized he gave me an extra fifteen hundred dollars. This dude had me straight tripping. I couldn't believe he was treating me so good and I hadn't even fucked him. I knew he was paid and the money he hit me off with was nothing to him, but still he didn't have to give it to me. The moment I walked through the door my moms was waiting with drool basically coming down her mouth. She was so thirsty for her money. I decided to fuck with her just to see how thirsty she was.

"You got my money?" she asked all common like.

"I need more time. I couldn't get it."

"I figured yo' silly ass wouldn't be able to come through. You been spending all that time wit' that boy and you can't even get no money outta him. I went in yo' closet and saw all those designer clothes he bought you. You betta take that shit back and get my money."

"I can't do that, I don't have the receipts."

"Well then go pack yo' shit up and get the fuck out my house. Go stay wit' that nigga you been fucking."

"You would really put your own daughter out on the street."

"You damn right."

"You really are a no good whore," I said as I tossed the ten hundred dollar bills to the floor. "Pick that shit up like the thirsty bitch you are." I went in my room, locked the door and blasted my music. My moms was truly a simple-ass trick. For the first time, I had to admit to myself that I was ashamed to be her daughter.

For the next few weeks, Azar and I grew closer and closer. One night when we were chilling at his crib, I decided that since he was never making a move on me, I'd have to do so. "Azar, do I look good to you?"

"Why you gonna ask me a silly-ass question like that. Do you think I would have you all up in my face if you didn't look good to me?"

"So why haven't you tried to have sex with me?"

"Because I can get sex from anybody, I'm not stressing it like that. I figured when you're ready you'd let me know."

"Well, I'm ready."

"You sure, Ma? I ain't in no rush."

"I know. But you've been so good to me. I want to be good to you." I did want to be good to Azar, but I also wanted to put all the moves on him that I learned from fucking Jamal. Shit, I didn't want to feel like I put all that work in with Jamal for nothing.

That night I put it on Azar. First, I gave him the best blowjob this side of Brooklyn. His eyes rolled back and his body jerked as I deep throated him. "Oh, Precious, just like that baby. Yeah, oh damn, baby," he said, moving the back of my head in a constant rhythm. I really fucked his mind up because not only did I let him come in my mouth, but I also swallowed. Then I rode his dick and when he screamed my name, I knew I had blown his mind.

Gangsta Lovin'

After putting it on Azar we officially became a couple. One day when he was dropping me off at work, he said, "Precious, tell Boogie this is your last day."

"Excuse me?"

"You heard me. I don't want you working here no more."

"Why not?"

"I really shouldn't have to explain myself to you, but since you're young, and this is new to you, I will. I don't want you at this shop no more. Too many niggas come through and I know they be tryna holla. One, because you fine as shit, and also because they know you my girl, they may try to get fly wit' they shit.

"I keep a low profile. The last thing I want to do is get extra 'cause one of these clown niggas steps out of line, or because you do. Enough said, so tell Boogie, 'peace,' and I'll pick you up at six."

I gave Azar a kiss goodbye, and that was it. He was right, though because I did begin scheming on getting two more just like him. With all the money Azar was now hitting me off with, if I had two other dudes to do the same, I would be sitting as pretty as a pussy cat. I already paid my moms up for four months in advance, but I was ready to get the hell out that dump. It didn't make sense to me to be giving her a thousand a month for some bullshit apartment, when for that amount I could be in my own crib.

Because of my age, of course, that would be a problem, but Azar had a hook up with a super, and he was working on getting me my own place. He suggested that I move in with him, but I told him my moms would probably try to have him locked up if I did that. My Moms stayed so high that she really didn't give a fuck if I was coming or going, but she would flip her wig if the steady money I was hitting her off with came to a halt. Soon I would be turning sixteen and it wouldn't matter no way.

One night after coming from Junior's for some banging-ass cheesecake, Azar said he needed to make a stop. He pulled up to the Marcus Garvey housing complexes. "Baby, you stay right here. I'll be back in a minute."

Although I lived in the projects myself and had been walking through them all my life, for some reason, I was feeling some type of way waiting in Azar's car in the dead of night. My stomach felt weary as I watched the typical corner boys walking behind the buildings with a crack head following to make the exchange, money for crack, hand to hand. There were other groups of dudes blasting they music, smoking blunts and guzzling down liquor, hitting on the local chicken heads, roaming the blocks. I was so caught up in checking out the scene that I almost didn't hear the gunshots that were ringing in the smoke filled air.

"Oh shit," I screamed when I zeroed in on Azar hauling ass out the building he went in less than ten minutes ago. From the one good light coming from the entrance of the project building, I had a clear view of Azar running with a big bag and aiming a 9mm at who I couldn't see. Before I could even think, Azar was coming around to the driver's side and all I heard was what sounded like an explosion as the glass from the back seat windows shattered.

"Open the fucking door," Azar roared as he pulled the door latch back and forth. He left the keys in the ignition when he ran inside, and I forgot I locked the doors the minute he was out of sight. I fidgeted with the unlock button because my nerves were shot. As soon as I heard the click of the door unlocking, I noticed the dude who blasted out the window getting closer to the car. He was just blasting out bullets like he was the terminator. I kept my head down as Azar put the petal to the metal and sped off, but not before he did, the dude blasted off one last bullet shattering the entire back window.

"Azar, what the fuck happened? Why that nigga bust off on you like that?"

I looked down at my hands, and they were shaking. I was trying to remain calm as possible in a situation like this, but inside I was freaking out. All it took was one bullet to end your life and that nigga who was chasing Azar had let out enough to kill a whole army.

Although my head was still down, I was giving Azar the third degree. But he wasn't saying shit. He was just hauling ass. Even with my head down, I was still able to look to the side and see Azar was sweating puddles. I stayed down for what seemed like another fifteen minutes until Azar came to a stop.

"I have to run up in my crib and get some shit. If you see anybody suspicious pull off and we'll meet up at your crib. But just drive far enough to get out of sight, then ditch the car and jump in a cab to take you home."

"Azar, I can't drive. I don't even have my license." I couldn't believe this nigga was trying to make me drive his car with no license and the back windows all busted out.

My hands were shaking, so I slid them under my thighs because I didn't want Azar to know how badly I was stressing.

"You'll fucking learn to drive tonight if need be."

"Why can't you just drop me off at home? This is some oh-other shit."

Then Azar lifted my chin and looked in my eyes real serious. "You my girl, I take care of you. You telling me you not riding this out wit' me?" he asked in the most serious voice I'd ever heard him speak in.

"Baby, I got you. Go handle what you have to do and if no one shows up, then I'll be right here waiting. If not, I'll see you at my moms' crib."

When Azar got out the car, I just shook my head in disgust. I didn't know what type of bullshit Azar was caught up in, but won't no nigga worth dying for. I was tempted to drive right out his life, but I knew Azar would find me and he might bust off on me for ditching his ass. It didn't matter now because in the blink of an eye Azar was back with three big ass bags he put in his trunk.

There was dead silence as Azar drove to his garage and pulled out his Range and left the Benz. I told him I wanted to go home but he begged for me to stay with him at the hotel room he got. Without him saying it, it was clear he could never go back to his apartment and needed to stay at the hotel until he came up with a better plan. That was cool for him but I didn't want to be on the run from some street niggas.

Hell, I still didn't know what had jumped off in that

building. But after Azar handed me 5 G's for what he called "Trooping it" I decided staying with him at least for the night, might not be all that bad.

I hardly slept that whole night. Then my stomach was growling 'cause a bitch was hungry. I wanted to order some room service, but Azar paranoid ass didn't want nobody delivering us food. That shit sounded crazy, but I was like whatever. He went out and brought back every breakfast item from McDonald's and I ate that shit up like it was my last meal. Finally after my belly was full, I bit the bullet and questioned Azar again.

"Baby, what happened last night?" Azar closed his eyes and put his head back. I figured that once again there would be a long period of silence. Then he began to speak.

"The moment I knocked on the door I knew the vibe was off. But I couldn't walk away," he said with frustration in his voice.

"Walk away from what?" I asked, feeling like I was pulling teeth trying to get an explanation from him.

"Man, I'm slipping. I thought them niggas shoot straight from the hip, but they shady. When the cat opened the door, and I stepped in the apartment, shit just went haywire."

"Damn, what happened?" I asked, now leaning closer, dying to know how shit ended in a blaze of bullets.

"So I step in, homeboy close the door and my new buyer start beefing about my product, saying the heroin I gave him was garbage. I was like, "Yeah, OK. Give me my shit back, 'cause I know this nigga lying."

"How you know he lying?" I inquired. This was the first time I ever heard a first hand account of a drug transaction going bad, my ears were plugged.

"Yo', I fuck wit' these Columbians. They got the best dope on the streets, hands down. So it's three of us in the room, and I'm eying these two niggas tryna get a feel as to what they next move gonna be. So then the nigga that's the farthest away from me start pacing back and forth saying he ain't got the product no more.

"So I'm like a'ight, give me my bread. At this point, I already peeped this black duffel bag on the side of the wall. My instincts were telling me my paper was in there, and I wasn't leaving without it. So I told the niggas you got two options: either give me my product or my bread, but I'm leaving wit' one."

"What did the dude say?"

"The two niggas looked at each other, speaking wit' they eyes, and that was my sign to pull out my heat. Them niggas had three hundred and fifty thousand of mine. Somebody was gonna be lullaby off that shit. I asked them one more time for my bread or my drugs. When I caught the nigga standing closest to me wink his eye, "I put a bullet right through it."

"Oh, shit, then what happened?"

"Yo, I blasted off on the other nigga, but instead of the cat I just shot falling back on the wall, his body fell toward me and he knocked my arm causing me to miss my aim. It gave the other nigga time to gain his momentum and he started busting off. I used his partner's body as a shield while I grabbed the duffel bag and fled. You know what happened next, the nigga left standing came at me wit' death on his mind. I know for a fact he and his people's gonna be looking for me."

I didn't even know what to say to Azar. I understood

why he had to go hard on those dudes because they were trying to rob him, but unfortunately he didn't finish the job. There is nothing worse than for your enemy to be walking the streets looking to get you. You got to spend the rest of your life watching your back unless you catch his back first. "So what you gon' do now, Azar?" I asked, doubting he even knew.

"Get the fuck outta Brooklyn for a minute. That apartment I was checking up on for you in Harlem should be ready in a week. I already paid the nigga. We supposed to pick up the keys tomorrow. But we can't move in until the end of next week."

All I heard was we, and I had already told Azar that my moms would shit bricks if she found out we was living together.

"Azar, you know my moms ain't going for us living together," I said feeling stressed about the whole situation.

"I know, but you'll be sixteen in a couple of months. We just won't let her know just yet. You can still stay there with her for the time being. Them niggas won't think to look for me in Harlem. I'll keep a low profile and see what the streets are talking 'bout."

The next day Azar and I drove to Harlem and picked up the keys to the new apartment. It was in a renovated elevator building on 142nd and Riverside Drive. Azar introduced me to the super as his girlfriend who would also be living there with him. Azar also gave me a bag and told me to hide it somewhere safe at my moms crib. He explained it was emergency money just in case anything went down. He also stressed the importance of learning how to drive and getting my license when I turned sixteen. So for the next couple of days, we drove out to this big empty parking lot in Long Island, and I practiced. Later on that day I stopped at home to hide the bag Azar gave me.

Luckily, in my closest, one of the floor panels was slightly lifting so I hid the bag under there and covered it with my shoes and boxes. I hadn't been home in about three days but my moms wasn't tripping, especially after I hit her off with an extra few hundred dollars and told her to buy herself something nice. I grabbed a few things and headed right back out. Azar was outside waiting for me, so I didn't want to take too long. He was still worried about coming through the Brooklyn projects. When I got back in the car, Azar was looking scared as shit. "Baby, is everything alright? You didn't see nobody did you?"

"Naw, I just don't like being nowhere around here," he said, driving off.

"Well, you the one who wanted me to drop off that bag at my moms' crib."

"I know it ain't yo' fault. You've been a soldier through all this." Azar held my hand and gazed at me for a minute, then he continued, "Honestly, Precious, I don't know what I would do without you. I really came off by having you as my girl. I can feel that you're loyal. That means everything to me, especially with the business that I'm in. Baby, you got me open."

Azar continued his speech until we pulled up to the Marriot on Adams Street. I felt he was molding me to be Bonnie to his Clyde, which wasn't cool with me at all. This was about getting money to pay off my greedy-ass moms and take care of myself, but now Azar had me caught up in some gangsta shit. I was mad about it.

When we got out the car and headed up to our room, I wasn't feeling right. It was like all eyes were on me, but they really weren't. Azar's paranoia was rubbing off on me, and that feeling wasn't good. Right when Azar was opening the door, he paused. "Oh shit. I left the bag in the car."

"We can get it later," I said, anxious to get inside and lie down.

"No, it's the bag with all the money I took from them boys. Baby, I gotta shit bad as a ma'fuckah. Will you run down to the truck and get it?"

Last thing I felt like doing was going back to the car, but I grabbed his car and room keys and walked away. I heard Azar scream, "Thanks, Baby," as I made my way to the elevator.

When I finally got to the ground level, the garage was deserted. It was quiet to the point that it was spooky. I hurried and ran to the car, grabbed the bag and sprinted back towards the elevator. As I waited for the doors to open, I felt the cold tip of steel on the back of my head. "Ain't this some shit," I blurted out. You know how you so scared you can't even be scared; that's how I felt. I knew that was a gun ready to blow the back of my brains out, but as bad as I wanted to cry, scream or run, I was numb. I just thought to myself, *Is this it? Is this how I'm going to leave this world, brains splattered in the Marriot garage?*

"I don't want to kill you," I heard the baritone voice finally speak. "If you do what I ask, then you can walk away alive. The choice is yours."

"What's the choice?" I spit, sounding more confident than what I was.

"All I want is my money and your boyfriend's life. If I don't get both, then I'm takin' yours."

"My boyfriend? Who my boyfriend?" I asked, wanting to see if he really knew who I was. I knew by asking the question I was trying his patience, but there was that slight chance this was a case of mistaken identity, although that was highly unlikely.

"Bitch, don't play wit' me. I saw you and yo' man, Azar, leave them projects a half hour ago. If I put my money on it, you was the same girl that was in the car wit' him a week ago when I blasted out his windows. I would hate to blast you now since technically you don't have nuttin' to do with this, but I will."

"So you saying if I give you what you want you'll leave me the fuck alone? I won't ever have to be bothered wit' you again?"

"I give you my word."

"Why you gotta kill Azar, though?" I asked, making a last ditch effort to save Azar's life. "Isn't the money enough?"

"That was my brother he put a bullet in. He gotta die. Enough talking. What's it gonna be?"

That decision was easy. I handed over the bag I just re-trieved from the trunk of the car. Then I handed him the room key, "Room 716." All this took place with my back turned away from him.

When he walked off, I made a quick turn to get a look at him. I only caught the side of his face, but it was one I would never forget. He had a thick, long, razor edge scar going from the top to the bottom of his chin. The elevator doors closed behind him, and I jumped in the Range and headed home.

On UPN's ten o'clock news they said that an unidentified man had been found shot once in the head sitting on the toilet inside his hotel room. I knew it was Azar and I actually felt bad for him. But what could I do? It was his life or mine. Like I said before; ain't no man worth dying for.

The next day I packed up my shit and moved to the apartment in Harlem. The money in the bag Azar asked me to hold was $50,000. I was going to use some of that to buy furniture for the place. I told my moms I was moving out but would still hit her off every month. That way she wouldn't try to cause no problems for me.

After I left my moms, I went to see Boogie at the detailing shop and told him how one day I was at Azar's crib, and he said he had to step out for a few but never came back. I explained that I believed some sort of foul play happened, and he was never coming back. I told him that Azar left me the keys to his Range, and he had two other cars at a garage.

Next, I made Boogie a business proposition attached with a favor. "Boogie, you can have all three cars. Take them to your friends at the chop shop and sell off the parts. That's easy money for you." Boogie had a lot of money, but he always liked to make more. It didn't matter how little or how much.

"Yeah, I can do that. Azar have some nice rides."

"Just so you know, a couple of the windows in the Benz got blasted out."

"What the fuck happened…don't even tell me. I don't want to know. So what do you get out of this, Precious?"

"All I want is a car of my own."

"You not even sixteen, nor do you have a license."

"Boogie, I'll be sixteen next month, and I'll be getting my drivers license."

"With a car you have to pay insurance, and you definitely can't park it in them projects you live at."

"Boogie, I got all that covered. Just get me the car."

"Alright. What you want?"

"A baby Benz."

"Don't you think you need to start off with a nice Honda or Toyota to keep your insurance down? Yo' boy, Azar, disappeared, so you don't have him to help you out. I could always give you your old job back, but it will probably cover the insurance and nothing else."

"I appreciate you looking out, Boogie, but I'm good. I won't have a note, so I'll be able to maintain the insurance. You also don't have to worry about the car being parked in the projects - I actually moved."

"Where?" he asked, curiosity written all over his face.

"I'll call you with the address when I get settled in. How long do you think it'll take to get me my car?"

"I need at least a month."

"Good. By that time I'll have everything straight on my end." I handed Boogie the keys and wrote down the address to the garage. There was no doubt he would come through.

As promised, Boogie hooked me up with a silver C240. It took a few months, but it worked out perfectly. It gave me enough time to pass my driving test and get my new crib in order. I also transferred high schools. I continued to hit my moms off, and she never questioned my whereabouts.

For the next two years, I managed to graduate high school and keep up my rent and all other bills. The super was mad cool. He questioned me a couple of times about Azar, but I would always say he was out of town. Then one day I pretended to be distraught and was crying right outside the hallway where I knew the super could hear me.

When he asked me what was wrong, I told him Azar broke up with me, and that I was devastated. By this time I was eighteen, so I was able to convince him to let me still stay and put the apartment in my name without a credit check. When I hugged him to show my appreciation I rubbed my ample breast against his chest and let him rub his hands down my ass. He was so grateful that he took an additional two hundred dollars off my rent every month.

It didn't really matter, though, because after Azar got killed, all I fucked with was hustlers. They threw money at me like it wasn't nothing. I worked my shit out so good that I still had a large chunk of the $50,000 that I was supposed to hold for Azar - that is, before he died. It seemed that every nigga I fucked with, I just got them open.

Just Me & My Bitch

It had been a little over two years since Azar's murder, but I knew this year was my time to shine. It seemed like overnight I went from living with my dope junky mom to flexing in my own fly ass crib with a Benz to match. I could come and go as I pleased, answering to nobody.

As I strolled down 125th and Lenox relishing in my ghetto dreams, I noticed a guy staring me down. I was used to niggas' mouths watering as they imagined how the insides of my pussy felt. When I reached the corner I stood in that 'I know I'm the shit' position. With my low waist jeans perfectly accentuating the gap between my slightly curved legs and five-foot-five-inch hourglass figure, the dude was in complete awe.

The closer the dude got to me, the more appealing I became. My butterscotch complexion glistened under the afternoon sun. The wind slightly blew through my wavy golden brown hair, which stopped around mid-back. My glossy lips added to my sensual looks. I'm sure the nigga felt he was supposed to have spotted me lounging on a Miami Beach instead of walking the grimy streets of Harlem.

"Excuse me, Ma, but can I speak to you for a moment please?" he asked in his most sincere voice.

I paused for a moment and ogled the stranger up and

down. I then folded my arms and smacked my lips before speaking. "Nigga, I'm not yo' Ma. Save that shit for the next bitch."

"Hold up a minute," he said as he reached to grab my arm. I instantly pulled away with my eyes speaking for me. He knew they read, back the fuck off. "I'm sorry, I didn't mean to grab on you like that, but I didn't want you to walk away."

"Hum huh," I said, rolling my eyes to let the stranger know he was getting on my last nerves.

"No disrespect, but you are far too gorgeous to be speaking with so much venom."

"Excuse me. Who the fuck is you? The Preacher's son?"

"Nah, my pops is dead, but when he was alive, he definitely wasn't a Preacher," he said with a devious chuckle.

"So why how I speak matter to you, since you ain't no savior?" I asked, hoping the nigga would keep walking.

"I said my pops wasn't a Preacher; I didn't say I wasn't a savior."

"How you know I need saving?" I asked, becoming more drawn into this slick talking dude's conversation.

"I don't see a ring on your finger," he said as he gently massaged my left hand.

"Maybe I don't want a ring on my finger," I snapped, pulling my hand away.

"All queens deserve to be blessed with the finest rings, and you are definitely a queen. If you don't mind will you tell me your name?"

"Precious," I answered in a silky tone, which was in contrast to my once gritty voice.

"Damn, your mother knew what time it was when you

were born, 'cause you damn sure precious."

"Cute, but I've heard all these lines before."

"I don't care about all those other cats that fed you lines. I'm a real 'G' so my line is the only line that matters."

Damn, this nigga feeling himself, I thought to myself. After getting over my initial attitude, for the first time I actually swallowed the whole essence of the man standing before me. His flawless mahogany skin was highlighted by a low cut, full of jet-black curls. He was six-foot-two and a solid one-ninety. His full lips were decorated with perfect white teeth. I had to admit he was fine. "So what's your name?" I said, warming up to him.

"Nico. Nico Carter."

"It's nice to meet you, Nico. So what you want from me?"

"Your company or maybe your hand in marriage, or maybe a pretty baby."

"Nigga, I ain't making no baby for you."

"You say that now, but just give me a month. You'll be begging to have my seed."

"You real confident with yours. What you pushing?" I asked, trying to get down to business. He was fine, but if he was broke, it didn't make a damn bit of difference.

"What you mean what I'm pushing?" Nico asked with confusion in his voice.

"You know what I mean. What type of whip you got?"

"Precious, that's not the type of question you ask a man when you just meet him," he said, sounding like a concerned father lecturing his daughter.

"He might get the wrong impression and assume you're a paper chaser," he added.

"Sweetheart, you got me confused with the next bitch.

I don't give a fuck what impression I give off. I don't fuck wit' broke niggas. A broke nigga make for a dry pussy. You feel me? So are you gonna tell me what you pushing, or do I need to keep strolling and go about my business?"

I knew every instinct in Nico's body was telling him to walk away and never look back at the danger standing before him, but being a typical nigga with a hard-on, his lust prevailed. "I tell you what, let me take you on a date, and I promise you won't be disappointed."

"I guess that means you not gonna tell me what type of wheels you got. I hope you not walking, because if you are, you'll be on that date solo." Nico laughed. "What's so funny?"

"You. Just give me your digits. You definitely gonna be my permanent piece."

I figured that instead of turning Nico off with my slick-with-the-mouth antics, I was pulling him further in. He probably wasn't used to my type, a woman so blatant with it. He had to respect the fact that I let it be known that you either come correct or don't come at all.

*****

"What's up, Maria?" I said, walking in the Dominican spot for my weekly wash and blow out. Maria responded with her standard nod and smile, which was fine with me since my beautician could barely speak English. After the deep conditioning and roller set I was under the dryer, dreading the hour process. Luckily, I came prepared with the latest magazines to pass time. I was enthralled in reading about the most recent rap battle between two of the hottest MC's when the rattle of someone pounding on my dryer jarred me from my concentration.

"What's up, homegirl?" Inga grinned as our eyes met. Inga and I had been cool since sixth grade, but in the last year or so we became real close. When I moved out my moms' crib and changed schools I would get lonely for female company sometimes. All the girls at my new school had established their cliques and looked at me as an outsider. Plus, they couldn't take that all they boyfriends was sweating my ass. Inga would come over and stay with me just about every weekend. We would just kick it together or go out on double dates since we both liked hustlers.

"Bitch, you was about to catch it," I said, giving her a pound. "I didn't know who the fuck was banging on my dryer like a crazy person. I should've known it was yo' wild ass."

"What you reading?" Inga asked as she sat down in the seat next to me.

"Just some rap bullshit. I'm starting to believe all this so-called beef just be a publicity stunt. These niggas will do anything for airtime."

"You got that right, and we be right there reading that bullshit like its gospel," Inga said as we nodded our heads in agreement. "So what's up wit' you tonight, you going to the club?"

"Actually, I'm supposed to be going on a date."

"A date? Who you fucking wit', Precious?"

"I ain't fucking wit' nobody. I just met this dude on my way over here, and we supposed to be hanging out tonight."

"He got money?" Inga asked, while rubbing her fingers together.

"I hope so, but if not, the date will end before it even starts.

44

If he don't pull up to the crib in some official shit, I won't have no problem telling him to forget my name and number."

"You got that right. It's too many niggas out here doing it to be wasting your time with a thirsty cat. But if he is rolling in the dough, hook me up with one of his friends. Truth be told, you know niggas making paper usually roll in crews."

"I got you. If he's official I'll turn you on. I haven't forgotten about that Jamaican cat you hooked me up with. I didn't even have to fuck that nigga; all he wanted to do was eat my pussy and take me shopping. A bitch was hurt when he got locked up, he was lacing me lovely."

"Yeah, he was real big on you. I speak to his cousin, and he told me that nigga still be checking for you. He even asked me if I could talk to you about going to visit him in prison. I didn't have the heart to tell him it would never happen. So I just said you went to visit your peoples down south for a minute."

"OK. What the fuck can he do for me behind bars, except tell me where he hid his stash?" I said, viewing my watch, seeing how much time I had left under this hot-ass dryer. I then looked back up at Inga, inspecting the shaky hairstyle she was rocking. "You came to let Maria do your hair?"

"Nah, I still have this weave. I'm tryn' to rock this until I get all my money's worth. I was on my way to the beauty supply store and peeped you in here and wanted to holla."

I couldn't help but think that Inga had got all her money's worth and then some off the tired looking tracks that were barely hanging on to her scalp. But I knew Inga's dollars were tight and she couldn't afford the necessary four to six week redo that was required to keep your weave fresh.

"Oh, that's cool. I was planning on hitting you later anyway. If my date is a bust, let's go shake our asses at the club tonight. If it's all good, I'll hit you tomorrow so we can set up a double date.

"That'll work," Inga said as she strutted out of the beauty shop.

*****

That night I got dressed for my date to the sounds of "The Emancipation of Mimi." Although I loathed that dizzy acting bimbo, Mariah Carey, I had to admit her CD was kinda hot. Nico already called and said he was on his way so I was just giving myself the finishing touches.

I put on my hot pink Juicy Couture terry cloth dress with matching shoes. I still didn't know if this date was going to even happen, so I wasn't stressing it too much. Since my apartment wasn't facing the street I couldn't even look out my window to see what type of whip he was pushing before wasting my time and going downstairs. When my cell phone rang again, I figured it was Nico telling me he was downstairs. No way was I giving him my home number 'cause he still was on my suspect list.

When I got to the front door entrance I tried to peep around to catch a glimpse of Nico's ride. All I saw was an old Chevy parked out front with the hazardous lights flashing. If that was that nigga's car, I was going to cuss him the fuck out for wasting my time. He had to know by just looking at me that it wasn't that kind of party. Then I heard my cell phone ring and it was Nico telling me he was parked right out front. I was so pissed I bit my bottom lip.

When I walked further out, someone beeped their horn and I noticed the hottest 2005 red SL65 AMG with banging rims. My face lit up like a Christmas tree. When I sat down in the car, the first thing Nico said was, "I bet you thought that banged up Chevy was mine," we both burst out laughing.

"You know I did, ma'fuckah."

"Seriously, Precious, you are way too beautiful to talk like that. Plus my name isn't ma'fuckah."

"I apologize. You know what I meant to say, Nico." I didn't mind giving him a little life cause his wheels were crazy and the nigga was even finer out his street clothes. He had on some top line Sean John shit. Not the sweat suit gear, but the slacks and button up shirt. His wrist was heavy with the Jay-Z limited edition platinum version Audemars Piguet watch. I was feeling his style.

"So where do you want to go tonight?" he asked, doing a U-turn in the middle of my street.

"Maybe dinner."

"You got a place in mind?"

"You pick the spot," I wanted to see what his restaurant game was looking like anyway. He jumped on the Westside Highway. We eventually ended up on Lafayette Street at a spot called Butter. The place was sexy. I was surprised because it was a white joint with a bunch of model type looking motherfuckers. It was cool though and the food was a'ight to be a white establishment. After dinner it was still early and Nico suggested we go to the movies. But I declined. I wanted to find out everything I could about him. So we drove to the park across from St. Nicholas Ave. and just talked.

"So, Nico, tell me about yourself."

"What do you want to know?"

"Everything." So Nico started from when he was a kid.

"My father got murdered when I was thirteen. Of course he was a street nigga. He used to hustle with my best friend Ritchie's dad.

"I've known Ritchie since I was three years old. He's like my brother. We grew up in the same projects and our mother's were best friends. After my dad got killed, shortly after, Ritchie's dad got locked up on some Federal charges and got life. With both of them gone I had to step up as the man of the house.

"I was determined to pick up where my dad left off, which meant getting my drug hustle on. One of my dad's captains took me under his wings and molded me into the perfect solider. But hustling was embedded in my blood, so I conquered the game with rapid speed. I have that deadly combination of intellect and street smarts. I can run circles around anyone that crosses my path.

"As I got higher up in the ranks, I tried to bring Ritchie in the mix, but he became withdrawn when his father got locked up. To make matters worse his mother got strung out on crack. Eventually it got so bad that he moved in with me and my mother, because his moms couldn't take care of him anymore. It took a few years, but Ritchie came out of his shell and we made a pact to never leave one another's side until death do us part." Nico paused and looked at me for a moment." "I can't believe I just told you all that. I don't even usually open myself up like this. But that's OK, because you are going to be my girl, I know it."

"Why you stressin' for me to be your girl?" I was curious to know. It was obvious that Nico was large and in charge. He probably had bitches throwing pussy at him from every direction. So I had to know what his fascination with me was.

"Besides the fact that you are unbelievably gorgeous, something about you is dark."

"Dark? What the fuck?"

Nico gave me that look. "I meant to say, 'What you mean.'" *This cussing situation was definitely gonna be a problem,* I thought to myself.

"That same look I got in my eyes, you got it in yours. I've never met a woman or man besides my father with that look."

"What look is that?"

"It's a combination of many things. The average nigga wouldn't be able to handle you, but I know I can and will. We are going to do big things together."

With the majority of niggas I fucked with, I wouldn't give them no ass until they had tricked a few G's on me first, but not with Nico. I willingly gave up the pussy that first night. It was crazy because no matter how hard I tried, he wouldn't let me get on top. That let me know he was determined to maintain control over me and our relationship. The way he put it on me, though I didn't have a problem with it. From that day on it was like that Biggie record, *"Just Me And My Bitch"*.

Hollyhood

Being Nico's girl was like being the First Lady. The streets bowed down to me as if I was their queen. I had to take it back to Brooklyn on a regular basis and represent my hood. See, Harlem wasn't my hood, I rep'd for BK. The first time I drove up to Boogie's spot in Nico's SL65, the place paused. They knew it was Nico's shit, and I had to be his girl to be pushing it. For everyone else who didn't know, there was no doubt in their mind I was some powerful ma'fucka's wifey.

I loved the stares and glares I received from dealing with a kingpin. Even for the people who hated on me, they didn't have the balls to say anything to my face. Nico's reputation preceded him, and no one crossed him, and since I seemed to be the closest thing to him, they didn't dare cross me.

Everything between me and Nico happened so fast. The next morning after we twisted each other out, he said I was moving in with him. He didn't ask, he demanded. He was so damn cocky, confident, and controlling with his shit, but it turned me on like crazy. I was open for it anyway. I agreed to move in with him, but I also kept my spot. As much as I digged Nico, I knew that any bitch that was about her business maintained her own crib. Nico had a couple of cribs, but I moved into his brownstone on the promenade in

Brooklyn Heights.

Anybody that is familiar with Brooklyn knows that is prime property. I'm talking million-dollars-and up cribs. I didn't understand how Nico maneuvered that, but that just showed how official his shit was. At first I didn't even feel comfortable being in the same neighborhood with all those rich pricks, and Nico could see how frustrated I was becoming.

One day he sat me down and schooled me. "Precious, understand something. The only way you become rich is surrounding yourself with rich people. I know this might seem like a bit much to you, but pretty soon instead of you worrying about who all these rich people are around you, they'll be trying to figure out who you are."

Nico was right. After a while a couple of ladies in the neighborhood would see me pulling up in my 6-Series convertible and would try to make conversation with me. They was curious about who I was. They swore down I was in the Entertainment Industry. When they got to asking me a million questions, I would slightly tilt down my Jackie O shades and say, "Sorry can't chat. I must be going," real Hollywood like.

I said to myself, *let it stay a mystery*. If I have anything to do with it, they will die trying to figure that shit out. It was bananas because in Brooklyn Heights, Nico and I were looked upon as a respectable couple who was just doing it, but the ghetto ran through our bloods. We both lived for the streets.

I didn't normally go with Nico when he was handling business, but this particular day on our way to do some shopping in the city we made a stop at one of the many blocks

Nico had on lock for a spontaneous spot check. It was his way of making sure his workers were doing their part and holding it down. Nico was the man, and when he pulled up in the hood with rims spinning all shenanigans came to a halt, and everyone stood in attention.

Although his best friend Ritchie was his right hand man, he didn't garner the same level of respect as Nico. The whole borough knew that Nico basically handed large portions of the business over to his best friend out of loyalty, not because Ritchie earned it, although Nico didn't see it that way. As far as he was concerned he and Ritchie were brothers. "How's it looking, my man?" Nico asked his field lieutenant, Tommy.

"It's all good. It's Friday, so you know the clientele is steady and the money is right," the stocky worker bragged.

"That's what I like to hear. I was checking up on you. You seem to have everything under control, so I'm out," Nico said giving Tommy a pound. "Hit me later with those numbers."

"I got you boss." Right when we were pulling off, Ritchie pulled up.

"What's up, my nigga?" Ritchie said as he knelt down on Nico's side of the car door. He then noticed I was in the car, "What's up, Precious?"

"The same thing, Ritchie."

"When you gon' hook me up wit' one of your girls?"

"I told you I don't fuck wit' bitches like that. The only chick I fucks wit' is Inga."

"Well hook it up."

"Ritchie, every time you tell me to do that shit you always cancel at the last minute."

"I tell you what. You and Nico come, we can do it fo'

sho' tonight."

"Why we gotta come?" I smacked. I knew Inga would want it that way, but I wanted to make Ritchie feel like I was doing his ass a favor.

"Com' on. Stop trippin'. It'll be fun, right?" He playfully punched Nico's shoulder, trying to get him to cosign on the outing.

"Yeah, it'll be cool."

"A'ight', I'll call her. We can go to the Harlem Grill. I heard they have some good food."

If I had to be bothered with Ritchie's silly ass at least I could get a good meal out the deal. "Put her number in your phone so you can make the arrangements to pick her up." After Ritchie plugged Inga's number in his phone, he noticed Tommy and told him to come here.

"Tommy, make sure you don't leave until all business is dried up. We don't need nobody slacking off," Ritchie said, trying to execute some authority. Tommy nodded his head as if agreeing with what Ritchie said, but I knew he gave it no merit.

From the few occasions I observed Ritchie, he had a way of making unnecessary comments in an attempt to make his presence known. I wondered if Nico ever picked up on that, but since he never mentioned it maybe he didn't. He had a blind eye when it came to Ritchie, anyway. Because I knew for a fact that Ritchie was straight jealous of Nico; it was written in his eyes.

"Man, you too lax with these niggas. They be coming at you like ya friends instead of your workers," Ritchie said with agitation.

"Nah, it's not like that. They know who's boss, but I

prefer for them to feel comfortable around me."

"Comfortable. Fuck that, you better make them goofy niggas fear you. They need to know if they step out of line it can happen."

"Man my temper is legendary so they all know it can happen. But fear brings about lies. Our crew is the eyes and ears of the streets. They gottta believe they can tell me anything, whether good or bad. Without the information from the streets I'm powerless. If that means making my crew feel at ease then so be it."

"I hear you, but I still say you need to put your foot in they ass every now and then," Ritchie stressed.

As I listened to them exchange words, I knew that Ritchie didn't understand that Nico had a different style of dictatorship. Ritchie's browbeating style actually worked well for many bosses in Nico's position, but Nico vehemently opted against it. See, Nico wasn't big on bluffing. If he had to instill fear in you, that meant your time was up, and your life was over. He maintained a calm, cool and collected persona that made even his worse enemies respect him. When the dark side of Nico appeared everyone knew to stay away.

"I'll think about what you said," Nico answered, trying to get off the subject. "What time do you want to meet up at Harlem Grill?"

"Nine is good."

"So we'll see you there, and don't have us waiting on you neither," Nico added with a smile, knowing how it was nothing for Ritchie to be late or not show up at all.

After Nico and I went shopping, he dropped me off at home so he could handle some business before we went out.

The moment my bags hit the floor, I called Inga. "What up?"

"What's going on, Precious?"

"Not too much. Did Ritchie call you?"

"Not yet, why is he supposed to?" I looked at my watch and saw it was quarter to five. "That nigga so simple. Yeah, he was supposed to call. The four of us is going to the Harlem Grill for dinner."

"Word...wait hold on a minute. My phone beeping." As I waited for Inga to click back over from the other line, I twisted my mouth up, thinking how slack Ritchie was. We saw that nigga at twelve in the afternoon, and it damn near five and he still hadn't called Inga. That's why he couldn't keep no girlfriend 'cause he was one of those simple-ass dudes. I could never comprehend why Nico had so much love for him. "I'm back. That was Ritchie on the other line."

"Oh he finally decided to call," I said sarcastically.

"Girl, yeah, he said he'll pick me up at eight-thirty. What you wearing?"

"Probably something I got today when Nico and I went shopping."

"Yah stay shopping. I hope Ritchie generous like Nico so I can start flossin'."

"I doubt it. I ain't neva seen Ritchie wit' no official bitch. 'Cause an official bitch wouldn't be able to deal wit' his clown ass on no long term basis."

"Well, maybe they ain't neva fucked him right. 'Cause he's a cutie."

"Whateva. Let me get myself together 'cause I been running round all day. I'll see you tonight."

When I hung up with Inga, I just rolled my eyes. Inga was my girl, but she always got so caught up in nigga's way before they started feeling her. I could tell by the sound of her voice that she was already feeling Ritchie, and knowing him, he was just looking for a big butt to bust a nut in.

Of course Nico and I arrived first and on time for our reservation at the Harlem Grill. The hostess led us to a table in the back. After our second drink, Ritchie and Inga came walking in the spot like they were on time. I knew it wasn't Inga's fault, but because she had a big Kool-Aid smile on her face from being so happy to be with Ritchie, she was guilty by association.

"What took ya so long?" I asked just to fuck with Ritchie.

"The traffic on the bridge was backed up." Inga said, already trying to come to the defense of her clown-ass date.

"Oh, it was moving fine when we were coming across."

"What ya want to drink?" Nico said, trying to keep the peace. For the rest of the dinner Nico and Ritchie talked, and me and Inga engaged in our own conversation. After finishing up there Nico took us to this DL spot called Zip Code.

Nico had to do a special knock just to gain entrance. He said it was an exclusive lounge for the top-notch hustlers. We stayed for a couple of hours poppin' bottles and listening to music. I stepped away for a few minutes to use the bathroom, and when I came back, Ritchie's hand was damn near inside Inga's coochie. She was giggling, and he was whispering in her ear. Right when I was about to tell them to get a room, Ritchie said they was breaking out. I gave Inga a hug goodbye and told her to call me.

"I had a good time tonight," Nico said as he drove us home. "We should all hang out more often."

"Baby, do you really think we should be making long-term dinner dates with those two? I mean how long can their relationship actually last?"

"Ritchie seemed like he was really feeling her."

"Yeah, feeling up her ass."

"Stop it. I'm just saying they seem to enjoy one another. It's cool. Inga's your best friend and Ritchie's mine. We have a nice little family thing going on."

I secretly hoped that Ritchie was so bad in bed Inga would kick him to the curb before anything started. As far as I was concerned, Ritchie was bad news, and I didn't want him in no family of mine.

"Let me ask you something, Nico."

"Go right ahead."

"You don't ever feel like Ritchie just riding yo' dick and not bringing nothing to the table? He always got some shit to pop about how you need to do this and how you need to handle your business like that, but it's all dead noise. That shit don't bother you, 'cause it sure as hell gets on my nerve."

"Precious, you too hard on Ritchie. Sometimes a cat has to throw his weight around a little bit in order to feel like a man, but it's harmless. Ritchie might have his shortcomings, but the reason why I keep him by my side is because he's loyal. With the game I'm in, that's a character flaw. These niggas out here ain't got no loyalty to nobody, but Ritchie got my front and my back." Then Nico turned and looked at me with a smirk on his face and said, "Listen here. I'm like a dog, I don't speak, but I understand everything. Ritchie is good people, trust me."

I sat there in the passenger seat, just nodding my head. The conversation was a lost cause. Nico was dead set on his opinion of Ritchie, which was disappointing to me. I always viewed Nico as a dude that was beyond reproach when it came to his street savvy. But if he honestly believed that Ritchie was a loyal dude, then he had the game all fucked up.

The following afternoon Inga called me, sounding like she was on her honeymoon. "Girl, that nigga Ritchie can fuck. He just left here like an hour ago."

"Where was yo' moms at when all that fucking was jumping off?"

"She went to Philly this weekend to visit her sister, so I had the place to myself. He's coming to get me later on this evening so we can go to the movies. Girl, I'm in love wit' that nigga."

"Whateva, Inga. You say that about every dude that beats that coochie good."

"Precious, this time was different. He was so gentle with me and before he left, he gave me five hundred dollars and told me to get my hair and nails done. You know it don't cost no five hundred dollars to get that shit done. He's feeling me, and I'm feeling him too."

I had to admit that I was surprised by what Inga was telling me. I always thought of Ritchie as being a five-minute fucker. I definitely didn't think he would lay up with a bitch or leave her money. Five hundred was a drop in the bucket for him, but the point was he gave it to her and told her to get her nails and hair done. Not only that, they were going on a second date already. Maybe Ritchie wasn't as bad as I thought. And if Inga was happy, then so be it. She deserved for a nigga to lace her. Now maybe she would keep her weave a little bit tighter.

"Inga, I'm happy for you. But don't get too caught up in Ritchie. I would hate for him to get you open, then break your heart."

When I got off the phone with Inga, I called Nico. I wanted to see if he had heard from Ritchie and got any feedback. Inga was my girl, and I would feel some kinda way if Ritchie played her out. Nico's cell went straight to voice mail. His phone was doing that a lot lately. For a second I wondered if the nigga was creeping on me with the next bitch but decided I was being paranoid. Not saying that Nico wasn't capable of cheating like any other man, but Nico knew he would have to be extra discreet with his shit. I do not play that. When and if Nico fucked around on me, it better be when he's going in and out of town.

Later on that day, I had an appointment at Boogie's detailing shop so I decided to stop by my moms' crib. I hadn't seen her in a few months, and even though I didn't fuck with her like that, I wanted to make sure she hadn't died of a drug overdose. I used my key, and when I opened the door, my moms was lying on the couch, butt ass naked with some dude on top of her. Empty bottles of liquor were around the couch and some needles and pipes were sitting on the table next to them.

For a moment I thought they were dead because their bodies were motionless, but then they both started moaning as they changed positions on the couch. I walked over to the stereo and blasted the music to wake the two junkies up.

"What the fuck?" the two of them said in unison as they jumped up off the couch. When I had their full attention I turned the stereo back off.

"Who the hell is you?" the bony Chris Rock look-alike screamed. He didn't look like new money Chris Rock, but 'Pookie' *"New Jack City"* Chris Rock.

"I'm her daughter, you nasty-looking crack head."

"Who the fuck you talking to?" the Pookie look-alike asked as he wiped the crust from his eyes and mouth. He motioned his arms towards me like it was about to be on.

"Nigga, I'm talking to you, and you betta watch how you speak to me. I know you heard of Nico Carter. Well, that's my man, and it wouldn't take nothing but a phone call to have your life ended, so back the fuck up." I had to put some sort of fear in the dude because junkies can be some of the stupidest, overly confident ma'fuckahs out here.

"Both of ya calm down. It's too early in the morning for this shit."

My moms was straight trippin'.

"It's two o'clock in the afternoon; the morning been ended. Now, my man," I said, pointing my finger at the clothes lying on the floor. "You need to get yo' shit and get the fuck up outta here 'cause I want to speak to my moms."

He looked over at my moms like she was supposed to say something, but I was still hitting her off with paper so she just turned her face away like her name was Bennet and she ain't in it.

I stood with my arms folded as the dude moved in slow motion getting dressed. He even tried to cover himself. "Nigga, ain't nobody checking for that little dick you got over there. Hurry the fuck up."

When he picked up his keys, he tried to grab the small amount of drugs they had left and my moms smacked his hand. "I paid for this shit. Get yo' hands off my drugs."

"Listen, we ain't 'bout to have no crack head fight up in here. Take that shit, Pookie, and get the fuck up outta here."

"My name ain't Pookie. It's Leroy."

"Whateva, nigga, just go." When I turned my head for

a minute making sure Leroy was gone and then locked the door, my moms tried to disappear into the bathroom. I went back there and started banging on the door. "Yo, I want to speak to you."

"Precious, damn. I'm shittin'. Give me a minute." Fifteen minutes later, my moms came strolling out of the bathroom like nothing happened.

"You a grown woman and can do whateva you like, but not on my dime. You're bringing any ole type of dirty niggas in here fucking them wit' no condom or nothin'. Are you tryna die of AIDS?"

"Just because you give me money, I'm still yo' mother, and you don't tell me what to do," she said, opening up the refrigerator and pulling out a beer.

"I tell you what then, how 'bout I don't give you no mo' money, and you do whateva the fuck you like."

"Precious, you know I need that money. You my only source of income."

"Then act like it. I would prefer if you'd check yourself in some sort of rehab, which I would gladly pay for, but if not, keep them dirty niggas outta here. You neva know. They might flip out on you one day and kill yo' ass. I know one day I'm gonna have to bury you, but I would hate for it to be over some shit like that."

"You neva know, Precious. I might have to bury you first." Something about the way my moms said that sent chills up my spine.

"Just do what I ask. Here, take this." I pulled out a wad of cash and counted out fifteen hundred dollars. I knew she would probably smoke it up in less than a week, but somewhere inside of me I wished my mother would get straight.

Every time I looked into her beautiful green eyes, I saw hope.

When I got in the car, I called Nico again, and this time he picked up the phone. "What's up, baby? Where you at?"

"Just in these streets handling business."

"Oh, I called you earlier and your phone went straight to voice mail."

"I don't know what that was about. Where you at?" He tried to change the subject.

"I just left my moms' crib. She was in there wit' some grimy nigga. I so wish she'd get off those damn drugs and get her life together."

"Baby girl, once a junkie always a junkie."

I knew the odds of what Nico was saying was true, but the fact that he said it bothered me. I was looking for a sympathetic ear, not a self righteous point of view.

"Have you talked to Ritchie?" I said, now wanting to change the subject.

"For a minute-why?"

"Inga said they supposed to go on another date tonight. Maybe you was right about them feeling each other."

"Oh, that's alright. I'ma see him in a few, and I'll ask him."

"Don't make it seem like you spying for me, so I can go back and tell Inga."

"I'm not. I know how to handle my man."

"So what time are you gon' be home tonight?"

"Probably late. I got mad shit to do. But I'll call you later."

My stomach was getting that queasy feeling which wasn't a good sign. The little bitch that's your conscience, who taps you on the shoulder when something is up, was doing a motherfucking tap dance on my shit. The message was clear: Nico was definitely creeping.

Although my instincts were screaming that at me, I needed some confirmation. I also wanted to find out the best way to handle it. The only person I trusted to discuss my suspicions with and who could give me sound advice was my main man, Boogie. I put my car in drive and headed to the detailing shop.

When I arrived, Boogie was in front checking out a customer's new Lamborghini, but he would have to continue that another time.

"Excuse me. I need to borrow Boogie for a minute," I said to the old-ass man who had no business pushing a sports car with all that speed. One wrong move on his stick shift and he would die of a heart attack. "Boogie, sorry for interrupting you, but this is an emergency. I'm sure the look of stress is written all over my face."

"Nah, I don't see stress. You looking like a Ghetto Queen to me," Boogie said, checking out my gear and bling.

"I appear that way on the outside, but on the inside I'm just tryna to maintain."

"From what I hear you're more than maintaining. I hear Nico is taking real good care of you. The streets say ya live like rap superstars."

"Oh, that's what the streets say? They saying anything else?"

"Anything like what?"

"You know, about what bitch is fucking my man."

"Precious, I know you ain't getting caught up in all the silly shit. That's the main problem when these men fuck with you young girls. You all get upset about irrelevant shit."

"What's irrelevant about wanting to know if my man is fucking around on me?"

"Because as long as he is taking care of home who really gives a fuck? You driving around here in the most expensive cars, designer clothes, dripping in diamonds and living in nice ass-cribs, but that still ain't enough. You gotta have a nigga's balls on a platter. I don't know what Nico is doing with his dick. All I know is that you are looking and living better than ever. Count your blessings and be done with it. If you start looking for shit on Nico you'll find it. Then you're going to cause a whole bunch of trouble for nothing."

"I hear you, Boogie. You know I always appreciate your advice."

"Good. Make sure you use it."

On my way home I replayed the conversation I had with Boogie over and over again. What he said made a lot of sense. I decided to give it a rest. Unless some shit about Nico and another bitch slapped me in the face, I would chill.

For the next few weeks I continued with my normal activities, except for hanging with Inga. She and Ritchie were kicking it hard. I was on my way to meet her at the Dominican spot to get our hair done, since we hadn't hung out in a minute. Inga was already there when I arrived. I was surprised about how good she looked. She had on a fitted white jersey jumpsuit that emphasized her small waist and bodacious ass. She took out her weave and her hair was cut in one of those classic Chinese bobs. It was hot because Inga's hair was jet black and it complimented her coffee-brown complexion. By no means was Inga on my level looks-wise, but she was holding her own. "Look at you, girl," I said, giving Inga a hug.

"I'm spending Ritchie's money right, huh?"

"Damn right. That outfit is slammin,' and I'm loving your hair."

"Yeah, Ritchie said he was tired of getting his fingers caught in my tracks when we be fucking. So I decided to rock my own hair."

"It look good. You looking real official, Inga. A bitch is impressed." After getting our hair and nails done, we stopped by Amy Ruth's for some banging soul food. Inga went on and on about how happy she was with Ritchie and how pleased she was to have a man that was taking care of her. I was glad for her too, although I still felt Ritchie was a snake.

"So how are things going with you and Nico?" Inga finally asked, after going on about her and Ritchie since the moment I met up with her.

"Everything's cool, I guess."

"What you mean you guess" Ya the Ghetto King and Queen. You should be on top of the world."

"I suppose, but between you and me, I think Nico cheating on me. I know all niggas get they shit off, but I don't think it's no wham-bam, thank you, ma'am shit."

"Why you say that?"

"Just a feeling, but I could be wrong." I could see Inga fidgeting and playing with her nails like she was nervous. "Inga, do you have something to say, 'cause you my girl? If you know something, spit it out."

"Precious, I didn't want to say nothin' because I thought it was just some hating shit by jealous bitches. But a week ago when I was at that beauty supply store, I ran into Tanisha and Vonda. We were just kicking it, and then they asked me about you. I told them you was cool and kept the conversation moving, but they kept going back to you. They told me that they heard Nico was fucking wit' this chick named Porscha from Queens. I honestly didn't believe them. I thought they were just throwing salt in the game."

"I'm sorry, Precious. Honestly though, they could still be lying, it may not be true."

"How did they hear about it?"

"Tanisha said her cousin is good friends with the girl Porscha, and she was bragging about how she was fucking wit' Nico Carter. She said she knew he had a girl, but she didn't care 'cause he had some good dick and kept her pockets heavy."

My stomach was now doing somersaults. I knew everything Inga said was true because I'd been feeling like Nico was creeping on me anyway. To have my suspicions confirmed had me nauseated. This meant the whole hood knew Nico was screwing this bitch behind my back. I didn't know how I was going to play this shit out.

"Inga, don't tell Ritchie we had this conversation. I don't want Nico to know anything about this until I figure out what I'm gonna do."

"No doubt, but honestly, Precious, this shouldn't even matter. Ritchie always talking about how strung out Nico is over you and how he never been like this over any other girl he fucked wit'. Forget about those other bitches. You know they just dying to walk in your shoes."

I listened to every word Inga said, but it didn't make a difference. My instincts had been right all along. Nico was twisting the next bitch back out and right under my nose. What had me really vexed was that the nigga was shitting so close to where he lay. I was probably the topic of conversation in every hood's hair and nail salon in the five boroughs. Nico had disrespected me to the fullest, and I had no choice but to teach him a lesson.

The Set Up

For the next couple of week's, everyday and every night I thought about the information Inga gave me. As bad as I wanted to put a knife through Nico's heart, I remained silent. I was spending every moment trying to figure out how to cause him the type of pain where he would wish he was dead, but he was very much alive. It was difficult though, because I couldn't just dump him and be with the next nigga; the code of the streets wouldn't allow that. The only dude I would want was someone on Nico's level, and all kingpin's wifey and ex-wifey were off limits. I also wanted to make sure my paper was intact before I bounced. There were so many things to think about. But the one thing I was sure of - a nigga was not gonna play me. That meant Nico had to go.

Friday night, Inga and I decided to go to Cherry Lounge because my girl, Medina did the party there. I was looking forward to drinking some bubbly and dancing to some hip hop. Nico and Ritchie were out of town, so Inga and I both thought this would be the perfect time to have some fun. The line was around the building when we walked up, but Medina was at the door and let us right in. Since we wanted to pop bottles, the lady that handled the tables led us back to the VIP section.

We were the only women with our own table in the VIP

section. We were surrounded by some recognizable street hustlers and music industry dudes. Before long, the place was packed and the crowd was jumping to 50 Cent and The Game. As I guzzled down my third glass of champagne, I noticed Tanisha and two other chicks I didn't recognize walking towards us.

"What's up, Precious? What's up Inga?"

We both nodded our heads, acknowledging Tanisha.

"This is my cousin Michelle and her friend Porscha."

I know the color from my face had to disappear. I was in shock that Tanisha had the nerves to bring the bitch that was fucking my man to our table. She deserved a good old-fashion beat down over that shit. I couldn't help but stare down who I somewhat considered my competition.

Technically, she wasn't competition because I was the one that represented as wifey, but because I was competitive by nature I had to look at her that way. I couldn't lie the girl was pretty and had a nice body too. We kinda had the same sort of look, except she was more hard-core looking in the face. I didn't know if it was due to age or just living a hard knock life.

"Tanisha, since yo' silly ass wanted to bring your people over here let's cut right to it. Porscha, are you fucking my man Nico?" I asked, looking her straight in the eyes.

"Excuse me?"

"Bitch, you heard me. You fucking my man, Nico, or what?"

"As a matter of fact I am, bitch," she responded adding a twist to her neck. Inga, Tanisha and her cousin, Michelle stood all frozen. They didn't know what was going to happen next, so when I jumped over the table and swung my champagne bottle at Porscha, I knew Tanisha instantly regretted trying to be fly and bringing her fat ass over to my table.

Right when the bottle was about to collide with Porscha's head, her cousin snapped out of her daze and knocked it out my hand. It didn't matter because I had two good fists that would finish the job for me. I threw my whole body on top of Porscha. She was petite so she went down like a thin piece of paper. I just kept swinging on the bitch. A right and a left then another right and another left.

The bitch was helpless. Right when her cousin was about to jump on my back, Inga stepped up and let her know to back the fuck up. Everybody knew Inga could fight. But the funny thing was, because of how I looked, the whole hood slept on me, but I was bout it.

Inga was probably the only person that knew I could fight my butt off, and that's only because I whipped her ass one time. I kept throwing the punches, then I took my shoe off and clobbered the bitch with my heel. Right when I started seeing blood the bouncers ran up and lifted me off the bruised and bloody hussy. The chick was in shock. Before the bouncers got me completely off her, I spit at the hoe and said, "Now go tell Nico I whipped yo' ass, bitch."

Luckily Medina was my girl, so they didn't try to get extra with it. They simply asked us to leave and told me I would be more than welcome to come back next week. Management was actually looking out for me because they weren't sure when Porscha finally got up off the floor if she would call the police and press charges.

Honestly, I didn't give a fuck because I would turn around and whip that bitch's ass again.

"Girl, are you OK?" Inga asked when we were walking to my car.

"I'm fine, but can you drive?" My adrenaline was pumping and the last thing I wanted to do was get in a car accident. About ten minutes into our ride home, Inga burst out laughing.

"Precious, you jumped over that table like you was part of the WWF. You put a beating on that bitch. I know they regretting they ever stepped to our table."

"I know, right?" I said, laughing too. I couldn't help but think about the scared expression on Porscha's face when I was pounding on that ass.

"Do you think she called Nico yet?"

"I hope she did, that's one less thing I gotta discuss wit' his ass. How is he gonna explain this bullshit away. That bitch sure had it coming, though. I wish I could've had five more minutes wit' her simple ass."

I slept until the middle of the afternoon the next day. I couldn't stop the dreams of beating the shit out of Porscha. Right when I was about to take my knife and slit her throat, I felt someone patting my arm and saying my name. When I opened my eyes, it was Nico.

"Baby, are you OK?" I shrugged my arm wanting him to get out my face and mad that he interrupted me right before I was about to end Porscha's life. "I came home as soon as I heard what happened."

"I'm fine. You need to go check on yo' bitch."

"Precious, what are you talking about?"

"Don't play wit' me, Nico. I know all about you and Porscha. That's why yo' phone always be going to voice mail 'cause you laying up wit' that bitch. Nigga, fuck you." I pulled the blankets over my head so I could go back to sleep.

Nico grabbed the covers and threw them on the floor.

"I told you about that slick-ass mouth of yours," he said, pointing his finger at me like he was scolding me. Now Nico had totally disrupted my sleep and I was wide awake, ready for war.

"I don't give a fuck whether you like what is coming out my mouth or not. You running round here fucking that cunt, and then the dumb bitch wanna step to me at the club. You lucky I didn't kill the bitch."

"Precious, I'm not fucking that girl. I barely know the chick. Whatever she told you was a lie."

"Nico, you must think you dealing wit' a straight fool. Who's the one that called you about the fight I was in?"

Nico paused for a minute because my question caught him off guard.

"Inga called Ritchie and told him, and then he told me."

I just nodded my head as I walked to my purse to get my cell phone.

"Who you calling?"

"Inga. I'ma ask her if she called Ritchie and told him what happened."

Nico grabbed the phone out my hand, so I went and picked up the cordless and he grabbed that too.

"What the fuck you need to call Inga for? There is no reason to get her in the middle of our shit."

"Bitch, you put her in the middle. You know damn well you didn't find out from Ritchie. That trifling Porscha called you crying the blues, and that's how yo' lyin' ass found out what happened. I'm done wit' yo' punk-ass. Go be wit' her, 'cause I won't have no problem replacing yo' bitch ass."

Nico grabbed me by my throat and slammed me against

the wall. His eyes were blood shot red and beads of sweat was gathered on his forehead. He was trying to instill fear in me, but the shit wasn't working. I could really give a fuck. This nigga was a clown as far as I was concerned.

"Precious, first of all get all that leaving and being with the next man out of your head. We family now. It's 'til death do us part."

I'm sorry I had to grab on you like this, but you was flying off the handle, and I need your full attention. Precious, I'm sorry. I did fuck around with that girl, Porscha, but it was only a couple of times, nothing serious. She was out of line for even crossing your path, let alone saying a word to you, and she will be dealt with accordingly. But, baby, you can't let these scandalous hoes come in and ruin our happy home. They just jealous and sitting around waiting and plotting to take your place. You smarter than that. You can't let that happen. I'm going to let go of your neck, but you have to promise me that you'll calm down and be mature about this shit."

I nodded my head yes to let Nico know I wouldn't black out on his ass when he let me go.

"So what you want me to do, Nico? Act like didn't nothing happen between you and that bitch?"

"Precious, I know that's easier said then done, but I'm begging you to be the bigger person and let it go. I promise I won't fuck with her ever again. I made a mistake. I'm a man. I can admit that. I'm asking for your forgiveness. I promise I'll make it up to you."

Nico's words sounded sincere but the damage was done. He would've been better off denying the shit to the bitter end. Now I knew for a fact that he played me out with the crumb snatcher, and he had to be punished. I already smacked Porscha upside her head, and I had no doubt that Nico would rough her up pretty good too, so she was taken care of. But if Nico thought he was just gonna slide through this like the snake that he was, he was in for a rude awaking. I would play along like it was all good in our hood, but a bitch was about to make a move, one that Nico would never forget.

For the next month, Nico bent over backwards, trying to make up for the Porscha fiasco. First, he bought me the new CLS500 that I was dying to have. Then he bought me a diamond-face Chopard watch during our trip to LA for a shopping spree on Rodeo Drive. I had never even heard of that street before.

I spotted all sorts of celebrities that I'd seen on television and in magazines. I felt like I was in Wonderland. Finally, we went to Antigua for a week, and while sitting on the terrace at our hotel suite, Nico got down on one knee and proposed with a rock that even Lil' Kim would have to respect. Even with all that, nothing had changed as far as I was concerned. Yeah, I accepted Nico's proposal, and as far as he knew, all was forgiven. But, I was secretly planning the demise of Nico Carter.

The day after we got back from Antigua, I got dressed and headed out that evening to a lounge called Rain. I had a seat at the end of the bar so I could get a clear view of my target. From what Inga told me, I knew that every Tuesday night around ten o'clock, Ritchie came here for a couple of drinks before handling his nighttime business. She also told me that as far as she knew, Nico never came with him.

About twenty minutes after I arrived, because I purposely got there early, Ritchie came sauntering in solo. I knew he hadn't noticed me, so I walked around the back in the direction of the ladies room. When I saw where he positioned himself at the bar, I walked in a path that he would have to see me. As I made my way closer to him, I pretended to be looking in my purse for something. When I got right in front of his chair, Ritchie grabbed my arm.

"Precious, what you doing in here?"

I put my head up as if in shock to see him.

"Oh, what up, Ritchie? I was supposed to meet my girl, Tina here for a drink, but she just called and said she wasn't gonna make it. So I just went to the ladies room, and now I'm heading out."

"Since you already here, why don't you have a drink with me? Unless you in a hurry."

I looked at my watch as if I might have some place else to be. "I guess I have time for one drink." Four drinks later, Ritchie was spilling his guts and had his hand on my thigh. I knew that fake-ass nigga always wanted to fuck me, so his behavior wasn't surprising.

"Precious, you know the only reason I fucked wit' Inga was to get under your skin."

"For real? Why was you tryna get under my skin?" I questioned as if I didn't know what was up.

"You always acted so damn uppity like a nigga was trash. I knew fucking wit' yo' best friend would drive you crazy. 'Cause in all honesty, I wanted you. Inga is cool, but I settled since I couldn't have what I really wanted. If you was mine, I would treat you so good, Precious." I would neva play you out wit' a tired hoe like Porscha. I told Nico what a dumb ass he was for doing that shit to you," Ritchie added, thinking that shit would impress me. Ritchie was a man, just like Nico, and he would put his dick in the next bitch too. I always knew Ritchie was jealous of Nico, and before I cared out of concern for Nico, but now I cared for other reasons. I was going to use it to play right into what I needed him for.

"I appreciate you looking out for me, Ritchie. I'll admit I was a little hard on you, but I think it was because I was attracted to you too. I did feel some kinda way when you started dating Inga."

"I knew it, I knew it," he belted as he slammed his fist on the bar. "Baby, I knew you wanted me just as much as I wanted you."

Ritchie was a bigger clown than I thought. Even though in my mind the relationship between Nico and I was over, he was still a way better man than Ritchie could ever be.

"Ritchie, why don't we leave here so we can have some privacy. I would hate for one of Nico's people to spot us."

"Fuck Nico. He don't run me."

"Baby, I know, but he is still my man. I don't want there to be no problems."

"If I have my way he won't be your man for long."

With that Ritchie and I exited the lounge. I followed him in my car as we headed over to his place. I didn't waste no time putting it on Ritchie. I planned on riding his dick real hard for a good ten minutes so he would cum fast, and then break the fuck out. But Ritchie wanted to try and seduce a bitch. He laid me on his bed and ate my pussy for about fifteen minutes, trying to make me have an orgasm.

I guess he thought it would get me open on him. But, unfortunately, he couldn't even eat coochie better than Nico. Trying to speed the process up, I started faking having an orgasm so he would get his head out my pussy. I had to be home in an hour, 'cause I didn't want Nico to start getting suspicious and asking me a million questions. Finally, we got down to it and I had that nigga screaming my name. Inga was right. Ritchie was working with a nice-sized tool, but he still disgusted me, so I couldn't enjoy it.

It didn't matter because this was work, so I treated it accordingly. He lasted five minutes longer than I expected, but once he came he was out like a light. After fixing myself up, I jumped in my car and went home.

When I got there Nico was still out so I took a shower and went to bed. The next morning I heard Nico on the phone yelling at somebody. He slammed his cell shut and threw it on the bed. "Baby, what's wrong?"

"Ritchie stupid ass. He was supposed to handle some shit for me last night, but he said he fell asleep. Ritchie's my right hand man. How the fuck is he gonna slack off when it comes to making money?"

"Don't get yourself so worked up. It'll be alright." Nico was sitting on the edge of the bed and I crawled over and began giving him a massage. "Relax."

"Precious, that feels so good," he moaned. "Yeah right there."

"Good. I wanna take your mind off everything," I said as I stopped massaging his shoulders and massaged his manhood with my mouth. He was moaning and pulling my hair tightly because it was feeling so good to him. I couldn't help but wonder if he moaned the same way when Porscha was deep throatin' his dick.

I couldn't front that shit was eating me up. I saw the bitch, and no, she didn't look better than me, and no, she didn't have a better body than me. But I had to question if she could fuck better than me. Only Nico knew the answer to that, and of course, he wasn't going to give it.

This was all the more reason I had to bring him to his knees, because this nigga had me questioning myself as a woman. And if the next bitch pussy was better than mine. That was too many things. But I would never share all these insecurities with Nico. This was pain I would bear alone.

My plan was to convince him that all was forgiven and forgotten. He would believe that all this drama only made our bond tighter, and no matter what, I would ride for him. That way, Nico will never be prepared when it all fell down.

Somebody's Gotta Die

Ritchie and I began having secret sexual tryst three times a week. If he had his way, it would've been everyday. He kept demanding that I stop dealing with Nico and be his girl. Ritchie had lost his mind. His ego and being pussy whipped was getting the best of him.

I was not about to let that fuck up my plans, so I had to constantly stroke his ego and tell him that I needed more time. He didn't even care that his friendship with Nico would be over, because he was never Nico's friend anyway. I explained to him how Inga would be devastated, and although he didn't give a fuck about Nico, I didn't want to hurt Inga. Which was true. Inga was just an innocent casualty in all this. When shit did blow up, I hoped she would understand and not take it personal.

"Where you going?" Nico asked as I grabbed the keys to my car.

"I'm picking up Inga so we can have a girls' day together."

"Oh cool. Call me later on."

"I will. Maybe you and Ritchie can hook up wit' us later and we can all have dinner or something," I suggested so I could get further insight into how their friendship was going, although I pretty much had an idea.

"Nah, that's not gonna work. Ritchie ain't been himself lately. We having major problems on a business level, so I definitely don't want to deal with him right now on a personal one."

"OK. I hope ya work things out soon," I said, leaving the room with a smile on my face. When I got in the car, I blasted The Game's CD and turned to track 17 *"Don't Worry"*, with Mary J. Blige. That was my shit. It's about a girl who holds it down while her nigga is locked up. That's the strongest kind of hood love. I thought Nico and I shared that, but he fucked it all up.

Inga was already outside, standing with a frown on her face when I pulled up. "What's wrong wit' you?" I asked right after she shut the door.

"Ritchie dumb ass. He been so anal lately. Every time I ask him for something, he bite my head off. He didn't even want to give me no money to go shopping. He only budged when I told him I was going wit' you. You know he didn't want to feel embarrassed and you run and tell Nico he's a cheap fuck. But still, I shouldn't have to go through all them type of changes. He don't hardly even fuck me no more. I believe that nigga might be open on some other bitch, 'cause his attitude is stank as shit. But whoever she is gonna be mad about it, cause I'm pregnant."

I damn near crashed into the dollar bus when Inga said that shit. "Pregnant? You sure?"

"Girl, yes, two months. I took the home test and went to the clinic yesterday to be sure."

"Did you tell Ritchie yet?"

"Nope."

"Inga, do you really wanna have that nigga's baby? You

just said ya having problems and you think he's open off some other chick."

"I know, but the baby might make him get his act together. Shit, we eighteen now. Most bitches 'round here 'un had their first seed by the time their fourteen. Ritchie and Nico are both like ten years older than us. It's time for them to start a family. I know Nico gotta be tryna make you have his baby."

"Yeah, but I'm not ready for all that."

"What you waiting for? Nico Carter is the biggest hustler in Brooklyn, if not New York. Not only that, he tryna marry you and you got that big ass rock sittin' on your engagement finger. You betta go 'head and have that nigga's seed. When I become Ritchie's baby mama, he ain't gon' have no choice but to take care of me and his child. I'm sick of living in these projects anyway."

"Damn Inga, I don't have a good feeling about this though. I don't know if tryna lock this nigga down wit' a baby is the right move. You might end up only fucking yourself. A nigga ain't gotta walk around wit' his belly poked out for all those months. Then when the load drops, you the one that gotta change them shitty pampers and stay up all times of the night until you get the baby back to sleep. All while Ritchie will still be running the streets and fucking mad other bitches, who ain't got no baby to watch. So while you think you trapping him, you only trapping yourself. And if you think that paper gonna be right, don't forget, at the end of the day, Ritchie is a street nigga. His money is illegal. It ain't like you got his Social Security number and you can take his black ass to court and ball out on a whole bunch of child support."

"I hear you, Precious, but as you know, I ain't gotta whole pile of options. I have a better chance of Ritchie staying with me if I have his baby. A nigga be having a soft spot for they first born, especially if it's a boy. Plus, girl, the baby will be cute 'cause Ritchie got that pretty hair. You'll see. Once the baby is born, he'll always have a reason to come back to me."

"Yeah, well, that's the same thing that every other baby mama living in these projects thought. But once little Ray Ray got about three and his daddy ain't nowhere to be seen, the only thing they be waiting on is that government check and food stamps. I would hate for you to be one of them, Inga."

"It'll be different for me. Trust me. Ritchie will come around."

The news that Inga just dropped on me could've easily put a monkey wrench in my plans, but I refused to let it. I told Inga from day one not to get caught up in Ritchie, let alone have a baby with him. Her stupidity wasn't going to interfere with my scheme.

After I dropped Inga back at her apartment, I stopped by my moms' crib to leave her some money and make sure won't no bum nigga residing with her. When I got to my car, another car pulled up beside me, and Ritchie was on the passenger side. The guy driving was on his cell phone. "What's up, baby? What you doing over here?"

"I was just buying some weed." I didn't want Ritchie to know that my moms lived over here just in case things didn't work out the way I planned. His silly ass might have come over, trying to shake my mom's down.

"Oh, I could've gave you some," he said smirking. "Am I gonna see you later on?"

"I'm not sure. Nico been trippin' about why I be gone so much lately." When I was about to say something else, I noticed the guy in the driver's seat flip his phone close. I didn't want no strangers hearing shit I had to say.

For some reason though, the dude seemed familiar to me, but I couldn't put my finger on where I knew him from. I figured he worked for Nico, and I might have seen him talking to Nico on the block. That was, until he turned his head to retrieve something from the backseat of the car. Suddenly I recognized the unforgettable scar engraved on the left side of his cheek. The dude probably didn't know who I was, because when he put the gun to the back of my head, my hair was pulled back in a tight bun. Right now, my hair was hanging loose and curly. I did my best not to let the shock of seeing Azar's killer show on my face.

"So you gon' try to see me, or what?'

"I'll definitely try," I said, absorbing all the crazy thoughts that were going through my mind.

"Yo, man, you seen that little bag of weed I had in the car?" Azar's killer asked Ritchie. Hearing his voice brought back my close encounter with death.

"Yeah, I put it in the glove compartment, but Butch, you don't need to be smoking 'round here. Them boys in the uniforms is out. Hold up a minute." *Butch, that's Azar's killer name*, I thought to myself.

"Ritchie, I gotta go, I'll call you later. I promise."

"You better," he yelled as Butch drove off.

I couldn't believe Ritchie was hanging with Butch. They had to be doing business together, but I doubted Nico knew anything about it. But whatever it was, it had to be no good. Butch was sheisty. The reason all that shit went down between him and Azar was because they fronted on his money and they stole his drugs. I needed to further investigate, and I knew exactly who to see. I went straight to the detailing shop to have a conversation with Boogie. I parked on the side until the last couple of cars were pulling off. When I went inside, as always, Boogie was happy to see me.

"How's my ghetto Queen?" he asked giving me a hug.

"I'm good," I said, not wasting no time. "I need to speak to you about something."

"Should've known. Follow me." Boogie escorted me to the back where his private office was. I didn't want to speak to him in front of the girl working behind the cashier desk. She could be the hood snitch for all I knew. "What you need, Precious?"

"Do you know a dude by the name of Butch?"

"Butch with the scar on his face?"

"Yeah, him."

"Yeah, I know him. I know you ain't fucking with that nigga. I heard you and Nico was engaged to get married."

"We are," I said, flashing my finger with the five-carat rock. "Just tell me what you know about him, Boogie."

"Bad news. He started off as a two-bit stickup kid, then graduated to robbing niggas for large amount of drugs. Somehow, even with his ruthless ways, he stayed in the game without getting killed and managed to come up as a major playa now. But real official hustlers don't fuck with him. He deals with a lot of these young boys that's coming up. Between me and you, some say he's the one that killed Azar."

That last bit of information I knew as a fact, and the rest just confirmed my suspicions. Ritchie was definitely up to something, and I had a feeling it meant bad news for Nico.

For the next couple of days, I tried to eavesdrop on as many of Nico's conversations as possible. Since he rarely discussed business with me, on my own, I had to see if Ritchie had brought Butch into the fold, or if he was still playing it close to the chest. He knew I wouldn't ask Nico about Butch, because then I would have tell Nico I saw Butch with Ritchie, and that would open up a whole other can of worms.

I considered getting the information out of Ritchie, but although he was a snake he wasn't stupid. I ask one too many questions, and the red flags would start going up.

Getting the inside scoop on what he had planned wasn't to protect Nico. It was to make sure it didn't fuck up my own plans. Whatever Ritchie was scheming on definitely meant danger for Nico, because in this business there could only be one king. As I stood by the double doors to the den where Nico conducted the majority of his business calls, the home phone rang. I knew it had to be for me since everybody called Nico on his cell.

"Hello," I said, irritated that my spying was interrupted.

"Precious," I heard what sounded like Inga's voice. She was crying and yelling at the same time. Instantly I thought that Ritchie sold me out and confessed everything to her.

"Inga, are you alright?"

"No, would you please come get me? I finally told Ritchie about the baby and he flipped the fuck out."

"Don't say no more. I'm on my way." I was relieved Ritchie hadn't blown up my spot, but I was also concerned about Inga. I didn't want to disturb Nico, so I wrote him a quick note telling him that I had to step out and would call him.

Inga was hysterical when I picked her up. "Precious, I can't believe Ritchie's foul ass. When I told him I was pregnant he smacked the shit outta me. Do you see this bruise on the side of my face," she said, pointing to a big red mark on her cheek. "He said he ain't gon' be trapped by a baby wit' a bitch he don't even want. Then he told me that if I didn't have an abortion, he would cut the baby out of me himself. Can you believe that monster?"

"Inga, I'm sorry. So what you gon' do?"

"I don't know. I really want to have my baby, Precious. Not just because of Ritchie, but I ain't got nothing else going on wit' my life. Having a baby will change all that."

"On the real, Inga. A baby ain't nothing but another mouth to feed. Do you really want that type of responsibility, especially since Ritchie don't want no parts of it?"

"Fuck Ritchie. I don't want nothing but his money to take care of the baby anyway. You were right about him, Precious. He's a snake." From there, Inga had nothing but diarrhea of the mouth. "I don't know if you've noticed, but lately Ritchie and Nico ain't been hanging. Ritchie been kicking it wit' some new kid named Butch." Before Inga had my attention, but after she mentioned Butch's name, she had my undivided attention.

"Who's Butch?" I probed to see if Inga could divulge any new information to me.

"Exactly," Inga said, looking at me to let me know we were on the same page. "I asked Ritchie the same thing, and he told me to mind my business. That made me even more curious. Last night when Ritchie thought I was sleep, I heard a knock at the door. At first I thought it was a bitch because Ritchie don't like nobody to know where he lives. I went to the top of the stairs being nosey, and I caught sight of a nigga with the most horrific scar on the side of his face.

When I heard Ritchie call him Butch, I realized that was the nigga he been on the phone wit' all the time. Precious, I swear them niggas was talking about fucking Nico over on some serious paper. I'm talking a million dollars. Ritchie tried to say that was a drop in the bucket for Nico, but it would start an all out war between him and some other niggas, because Nico don't take nobody getting over on him and his money."

It was all making sense now.

"Ritchie was trying to take Nico out without getting any blood on his own hands. Butch was his partner in all this. They probably had big plans to run every block Nico had on lockdown together."

"When was all this supposed to be going down?"

"I'm not sure, and after the fight we got into this morning, I have no way of finding out. But you betta warn Nico that Ritchie's slimy ass is out to get him."

"I will," I said, knowing I had no intentions of alerting Nico to the information. "With the dime you just dropped on me, I need to get home and talk to Nico. Here's some money so you can stay at a hotel for a couple of days and get some other things you might need."

"Thanks, Precious," Inga said as I handed her eight hundred dollars.

"Inga, keep a low profile for the next few days, and if you speak to Ritchie, don't lose your cool and tell him any of the shit you just told me."

"I got you."

Right after I dropped Inga off at the hotel, my cell started ringing and it was Ritchie.

"Hello."

"Baby, what up?"

"You tell me."

"You, me. I want to take you on a vacation this weekend."

"Ritchie, I would love to, but you know Nico ain't having it." Today was Sunday, which meant Ritchie planned on having Nico out the way by the end of the week if he was planning a vacation with me.

"Baby, do you love me?"

"Ritchie, you know I do."

"Then let me handle Nico. Just be ready to leave Friday."

"Well, can I see you tonight? I miss you."

"I'ma be tied up for the next couple of days, but definitely Friday. But I'll call you."

I began wondering exactly when Ritchie started planning the murder of his best friend. Was it before or after he fell in love with the pussy? Right now it didn't matter. I had to come up with something fast. I had been waiting to drop the bomb on Nico when I had a hundred thousand dollars stashed, but now I had an opportunity to walk away with a cool million. With that type of money, I could leave Brooklyn and start my life over.

I was relieved when I saw Nico's car parked outside. I needed to pick his brain to see if he had any idea that Ritchie was plotting to set him up. Nico didn't hear me when I came inside, so I walked quietly where I could hear him clearly on the phone from the den. The door was open, so I stood on the side of the wall.

He was saying something about this new diesel connection Ritchie hooked him up with, and they had the potential to make a shit load of money together. He went on to say that the first go round, he was starting small with just a million worth to see how good their product sells on the streets. Then he told whoever he was talking to that he had a lot of moves to make tonight so could he stop by the warehouse and bring him the million over and he would keep it at his crib since he and Ritchie were hooking up early tomorrow to meet with the new connect and make the exchange.

I knew exactly where Nico kept his money stashed. He usually had no more than fifty thousand dollars in the house, but I guess he figured that the million would only be here overnight so it didn't matter. This was working out better than I'd hoped. As Nico finished up his call, I tiptoed upstairs so he wouldn't think I heard anything.

When Nico finally came upstairs, I was just getting out the shower and he was obviously surprised to see me.

"Baby, I didn't even know you were home," he said as I saw his dick rise up from looking at my naked wet body.

"Oh. When I got home I didn't see you so I just came up here to take a shower and go to bed. I'm a little tired."

"I hope not too tired to let me get inside of you." Nico picked me up and led me to the bed. I decided to put it on him extra good since it would be the last time he'd ever feel the inside of my pussy. After we finished, I had to admit that nobody could fuck me like Nico, but oh well, sex isn't everything.

Right when I stood up to go to the bathroom, I heard the door bell ring. "Baby, you want me to get the door."

"Nah, that's just Tommy dropping off some paperwork. I'll be back."

Yea, some paperwork in the form of a million dollars, I thought to myself. It didn't take long for Nico to come back upstairs. "That was fast."

"I told you Tommy just had to drop off some paperwork."

"Oh. You wanna go to the movies tonight?" I asked, knowing he already had plans but wanting to see what they were.

"Baby, I can't tonight but maybe tomorrow."

"Oh, you hanging out wit' Ritchie?"

"Nah, I have some business to handle."

"How are things between ya anyway, is there still tension?"

"Everything is cool. We worked it out. Ritchie snapped out of whatever funk he was in. You know we brothers; it's 'til death do us part."

When Nico finally headed out, I immediately started getting my shit together because I was working on borrowed time. I wasn't sure if I was going to be able to come back for the rest of my belongings so I gathered up as much of my stuff as I could in order of importance, starting with all my jewelry (including Nico's), furs, designer bags, shoes and then clothes. Once I got all that in the car, I went in the basement where Nico kept his money. He had no idea I knew where he stashed it since I never came down here. I actually found it by accident when Nico was out of town and there was a power outage. At that time, when I went in the basement with the flashlight, I tripped and found the box switch, and the money and a gun. There wasn't much paper so I left it there. Plus, I didn't want Nico to know I knew just in case I had to take it for whatever reason in the future.

Well, that reason had presented itself. The money was wrapped in bundles stashed inside a duffel bag. I grabbed it and the gun just in case I needed protection. After doing one more house search to make sure I wasn't forgetting anything, I headed out.

When I got in the car, I called Inga to see if she heard

from Ritchie and she told me no, so then I called him. When he answered he sounded like he was in the middle of something. "Ritchie, I need to see you."

"Precious, I'm busy right now. You gonna have to wait."

"I can't. It's important. It's about Nico."

"Oh shit. Did you tell him about us?"

"Listen, I need to see you," I said, not giving anymore information so he would bring his ass on.

"Alright, meet me at my crib in a half."

I knew he was shittin' bricks, hoping I didn't blow his spot to Nico and mess up the bloodshed he was plotting to start on his own. Luckily, it was dark outside so I parked my car across the street waiting for Ritchie to come home. When he pulled up I immediately called Nico.

"What's up, Baby?" Nico said, when he answered the phone.

"I was calling to tell you bye."

"What you mean, 'bye'? Where you going?"

"I can't do this no more, Nico."

"Do What? Stop talking in riddles, Precious."

"After we got back from Antigua I tried to put the whole Porscha situation behind me, but I couldn't. The only person that was able to console me was Ritchie."

"What the fuck did you say?"

"Nico, I've been seeing Ritchie for a few months now, and we're in love. I'm pregnant and the baby is his," I said with a slight sniffle in my voice as if holding back tears.

"Precious, don't fucking play with me. This shit ain't funny."

"It's not meant to be. I've packed my stuff. I'm leaving you."

"Where the fuck are you right now?"

"On my way to Ritchie's."

"I'm going to give you one more chance to take all this bullshit back before I lose it."

"I can't take it back, Nico, 'cause it's the truth. Why do you think Ritchie was showing you so much shade? He couldn't stand the fact that I refused to leave you. But once I found out I was pregnant, I decided it was time to let you go."

"That might be my seed. How you know I'm not the father?"

"I just know," I said, sounding confident.

"Then you a dead bitch," Nico said and hung up the phone.

I pulled my car in front of Ritchie's house in plain view for Nico to see. I then walked across the street and hid beside a house under construction.

Within fifteen minutes, Nico flew down the street and jumped out his truck with gun in hand. He paused for a quick second at the side of my car and kicked it before running up Ritchie's front stairs. He banged on the door with gun drawn, and when Ritchie opened it probably thinking it was me, all I heard was Nico screaming, "Where the fuck is Precious at?" before the door slammed shut.

I was waiting to hear the first gunshot before I placed my next phone call, when I noticed a familiar looking car coming down the street. When I realized it was Butch, I had to act fast. There was no way I could let him interfere with what was going on in Ritchie's crib. I snuck around the back of the house under construction and ducked behind another car before sneaking across the street. I waited until Butch got under the darkness of Ritchie's walkway before I stopped him.

"Excuse me, Butch, but where do you think you going?"

He turned around slowly and from the streetlight he tried to get a look at my face. "Who are you?"

"I'm sure you don't remember me, but I'll neva forget your face." I had my hands behind my back, holding the gun I took from Nico.

Butch's intuition start kicking in and he knew by the expression on my face I wasn't happy to see him. He instinctively put his hand in the back of his pants, feeling for his own gun.

"Looking for something? Outta all the times to forget your girl, you picked the wrong occasion. This is for Azar, bitch," I said as I raised my gun and let off three shots to the chest.

As the bullets exploded leaving golfball sized holes in his body, Butch finally fell backwards, landing on the bottom step. I walked up to him and put one more bullet in his face for good measure.

Right then I heard the shots I had been waiting for ringing out of Ritchie's house. I left Butch leakin' on the side of the curb, ran to my car and dialed 911 from a burner I purchased as I drove off. "Yes, I heard several gunshots coming from 218 Adelphi Street. I think somebody might have been murdered."

My heart was beating so fast. It wasn't because I had just killed somebody; it was just the excitement of seeing my plan come together. I prayed that the gunshots I heard coming from Ritchie's house were that of Nico murdering him. If they weren't, everything would be ruined. I wanted Ritchie dead and Nico alive to suffer being locked up.

Patiently Waiting

Before I was two blocks away from Ritchie's house, I saw police cars speeding down the street. I knew within minutes the street would be blocked off, and at least one murder investigation would be underway, hopefully two. Although I liked having the gun I took from Nico for protection, I had to get rid of it now since Butch's body was on it and probably a few more.

I drove across the bridge to the city and tossed the gun in the Hudson River. I then drove back to Brooklyn and went to the hotel where Inga was staying. By this time it was midnight, but I knew Inga stayed up late. When I knocked on her room door, she was up watching a movie and munching on snacks.

"Girl, I was surprised when you called saying you were on your way over. Nico gon' start trippin' if you don't go home soon."

"I know, so I'm not gonna stay that long. I just wanted to bring you something."

"What?"

"Take this," I said, handing her an envelope I had in my Louis Vuitton backpack. Her mouth dropped when she opened the envelope and saw all the money. "That's fifty thousand dollars to maintain yourself for a minute. Here are the keys to my apartment on Riverside Drive. I already paid the rent up for a year so you don't have to put no money towards that. Honestly, Inga, I don't want you to have Ritchie's baby for a lot of reasons, but if you decide to, this will give you a start."

"Damn, Precious, you some type of friend," Inga said, giving me a hug.

"Well, I better be going. You know how Nico can get."

I walked out of that hotel room not knowing when I would see Inga again. I didn't give Inga that money because I felt guilty about fucking with Ritchie. I just wanted her seed to be OK. I knew Inga would have that baby because she didn't understand the survival of the streets. Just because you come from the projects and see how hard it is to have something, it doesn't mean you comprehend the struggle. Inga never understood, but I hoped with the money I gave her and the crib, she would try to give her baby a better life than the one we had growing up.

I needed to get out of Brooklyn fast, so I took it over to Jersey. I'd only been there a couple of times, but I did remember it was nothing like New York. I checked in at the Hyatt Regency in Jersey City. When I got in my room, it had a banging view of the Hudson River, and I thought about Butch's murder weapon being somewhere in that big body of water.

I then got undressed, and since it was too late to watch the news, I took a hot shower and fell into a deep sleep. I didn't wake up until late in the afternoon, and the first thing I checked was my cell phone. I had no missed calls or messages. I opened my door to get the paper, but it was just the local *Star Ledger*. They definitely wouldn't have Brooklyn news in there. Nothing was on television but soaps, *"Judge Mathis"* and talk shows. Waiting to see what happened was driving me crazy. I ordered room service thinking that eating some food would minimize my anxiety. Two more hours passed, and I decided I needed some fresh air. I also needed to find a storage place and meet up with a guy I knew to get another gun. With all the drama I had going on, it was imperative for me to keep protection on me.

Finding a place to put all my stuff until I figured out my next move was first on my list. I located a Storage USA and went in to fill out the application. Once I got the spot, I purchased a lock and put the majority of my belongings in there, including my money. Last thing I wanted was to be caught with a million dollars, plus that shit felt like a ton of bricks.

Then I headed over to Harlem to meet up with this dude named Smokey. I used to fuck with one of his homeboys, but after he got locked up we still remained cool. Any weapon you needed, he could hook you up. I purchased another 9mm since I felt comfortable handling it, said my piece and broke out.

By the time I got back to my room, still no calls. I turned on the television to catch the six o'clock news not feeling optimistic I would find out anything, but then my patients paid off:

"This is Steve Douglass reporting live from Fort Greene. The house behind me," he turned, pointing his finger at what looked to be Ritchie's house, "Is the crime scene of a double homicide that occurred late last night in this upscale section of Brooklyn."

I held my breath, waiting to see who was the second person killed.

"The two male victims have yet to be identified, but the cops do have a suspect in custody. His name is Nico Carter, a purported notorious drug kingpin."

Not caring to hear anything else I switched off the television and flopped down on the bed. "Hallelujah," I echoed as I spread my entire body across the bed. I finally felt some sort of justice. Even so, I wouldn't be completely satisfied until Nico was doing life behind bars. In one night I was able to get rid of the three people I hated most in this world. But the punishment Nico would soon endure was the sweetest. If the system prevailed, he would spend the rest of his life locked up, knowing his fiancée was fucking his best friend behind his back, and believing that I was actually pregnant by Ritchie. That was enough to make any man want to get a hold of a bed sheet and hang himself inside his jail cell. Nico had too much pride to ever commit suicide, so he would have no choice but to spend his days and nights in confinement visualizing Ritchie twisting my back out and wondering if I screamed his name and called him daddy the way I did with him. Good for that motherfucker.

I was surprised that still nobody called me about Nico. I knew the streets had to be buzzing. The only person I really expected to call me was Inga. Boogie would never discuss that shit with me over the phone, so I decided to go see him first thing in the morning. He always got to work an hour before business officially opened. That night I went to bed early because tomorrow was going to be a long day.

When I arrived at Boogie's shop early in the morning, the door was locked. I knew he was the there because his red Deville was parked out front. I knocked for five minutes before he came to the door.

"What you doing here?" he questioned with a surprised look on his face. "I'd think you be at home waiting on a collect call from Nico."

"I haven't been staying there. I don't know exactly what went down, so I've been keeping on the low. That's why I came to see you, Boogie," I said, squeezing past him since he was blocking the door entrance.

"Sorry 'bout that," Boogie said, realizing I damn near had to knock him over to get inside. "From what I hear, it's not looking good for Nico. Supposedly the cops caught him at the scene of the crime with the murder weapon."

"On the news I saw that the murders took place at Ritchie's house, but they didn't say who the victims were."

"You haven't spoken to Nico?"

"No, I told you I haven't been home. The night it happened, Nico and I got in an argument, so I stayed at a hotel. I just heard about the murders yesterday."

"One of the men was Butch and the other one was Ritchie."

"Ritchie," I shrieked as if in shock. "Are the streets saying why?" In my mind I was finding it difficult to act as if this was all new to me. I hoped that Boogie didn't pick up on it.

"Word has it that Ritchie was working with Butch to cross Nico on some underhanded shit. Nico got word of it and finished them both off. What's puzzling is how Nico was so sloppy with it. He got many niggas on his payroll that murder for him like this," Boogie said, snapping his two fingers together. "Why he did the shit himself I have no idea. One thing I do know, it's not looking good for Nico Carter."

"Has he had a bail hearing?"

"I doubt it, but even so, they not setting no bail for that man. The local, state and Federal government has had a hard-on for Nico for so many years. Never did they think they would get him for murdering his best friend. If they have their way, Nico Carter won't ever see the light of day."

"Thanks for the insight, Boogie, but I gotta be going. I need to stop by the house and pick up some things."

"You're taking this pretty well, Precious. You have to be worried about how you're going to maintain with Nico behind bars."

"Not really. Financially I'll be straight, especially if you help me out."

"What, you want your old job back?"

"That's funny, Boogie. You know I'm way past that."

"I thought so too, but how else can I help you?"

"I have some money stashed away, but I need to make it legitimate."

"Legitimate how?"

"You know, like a bank account. Maybe buy a house."

"A house? How much money we talking about?"

"A million dollars."

"How in the hell did you get hold of a million dollars? I don't want to know. The less I know the better. I'll help you, Precious, but it's gonna cost you."

"I know Boogie, this is business and you always want your cut."

"No doubt. I'll place a few phone calls. I should know something by tomorrow so stop back through in the evening around closing."

"Don't let anyone know you've seen me, Boogie, or about the million dollars."

"Who you trying to school? I know how to handle business."

I gave Boogie a slight smile because he was the original playa in all this.

"By the way, how did the cops catch Nico at Ritchie's house?"

"An anonymous tip. I guess somebody had it in for Nico."

"I guess so," I said, walking out the door.

I was relieved to know that Nico hadn't leaked to the streets why he really killed Ritchie. Or maybe he hadn't spoken to anybody to inform them. But Nico was so private, he rarely confided in anybody. Besides me, the closest person to him was Ritchie. He had no family. Right before I met him, his mother passed away. The only family he probably had right now was his attorney.

I decided that I would drive past our brownstone to see if the cops had blocked it off. I slowed down at the far end of the corner. There was no indication that the cops had shut it down, so I proceeded with caution moving forward.

Right then I noticed Tommy coming out the house, empty-handed. I wondered if he'd spoken to Nico and came to retrieve the million dollars, or did he take it upon himself to get his hands on the money because Nico was locked up. I debated whether or not to pop up on him, but if he did speak to Nico, there was no telling what he was told to do to me.

When Tommy got in his truck and drove off, I left my car on the corner and crossed the street to do my own investigating. As I got closer to the front stairs, I immediately noticed the basement window was busted open. I wondered why our state-of-the-art alarm system didn't go off when it happened, but I quickly remembered that when I bolted out the house that night, I forgot to turn it on. That motherfucker Tommy didn't come on Nico's orders, he came to rob him. The reason I knew this was because if Nico had spoken to Tommy directly, he would've let him know where he kept the spare key hidden so he didn't come in this neighborhood busting windows out and possibly drawing unnecessary attention to himself.

Without a second thought, I turned right back around and got in my car. Before I could finish my thoughts, my cell phone started ringing and it was Inga. "What's up, Inga?" I said calmly. I wasn't in the mood to speak to her, but I needed to hear as much street gossip as possible.

"Precious, did you hear about Ritchie?" Inga bawled. By the tears that were obviously flowing, she sounded as if she just heard about the murders.

"Yeah, you just hearing about it?"

"Hmm hun. That night when I saw you, the next morning I had to go to the hospital. I was having real bad cramps in my stomach and there was a little bit of blood. I just got out today."

"Did you lose the baby?" I prayed the answer would be yes.

"No, the baby is fine. The doctor told me I'ma have to take it easy throughout my pregnancy."

"With Ritchie being dead you still want to have his baby?" I asked while saying to myself, this *is a dumb bitch.*

"Yeah. I know Ritchie was foul, but I loved him. I guess you told Nico that Ritchie was tryna to set him up. That's why he killed him."

"Inga, I neva even had a chance. When I got home that night, Nico was already gone. I didn't even know what happened until I heard it on the news."

"Well, he must of found out some other way. Ritchie's stupid ass should've neva crossed Nico. But I can't believe Nico's in jail, you must be devastated, Precious. I know how much you love him."

"So much is going on I really haven't had time to take it all in."

"Have you spoken to Nico?"

"No, I haven't been staying at home. I wasn't sure if the cops was gonna run up in there or something."

"That's true. I heard Nico's supposed to have a bail hearing tomorrow morning. From what I hear, they doubt he gonna get bail."

"Where you hear that from?"

"This girl named Vanika."

"Who that?"

"She Corey's sister. Corey's a little nigga. He works for one of Nico's street lieutenants."

"What else she say?"

"Not too much. Just that everybody stressed 'cause wit' Nico locked up and Ritchie dead; they don't have nobody to lead the way. Them two was the only ones that dealt one on one wit' the connect. Ain't nobody heard from Nico. They don't know if the police ain't letting him make no phone calls or what. That's why I was wondering if you spoke to him."

"Not yet."

"So are you gonna go to court for his bail hearing tomorrow?"

"I don't know. Nico might want me to keep a low profile."

"That's true. Wit' Nico locked up I'll understand if you'll need your apartment back."

"Nah, don't worry about it. I'll make some other arrangements."

"I know you ain't going back to your moms' crib."

"Nope." Inga had me feeling she was the police with all these simple-ass questions she was spitting at me.

"So what do…"

"Yo, I gotta go. I'll be in touch," I said, abruptly ending the call. There was nothing left to discuss with Inga because she gave me all the pertinent information she had. The rest of the conversation would've consisted of her picking my brain, which was out of the question.

The first thing I did when I got back to the hotel room was turn to the news. I knew they probably wouldn't have any new information about the case, but I had to do something to calm my nerves. I was pacing the floor back and forth, wondering if I should go to court in the morning. I prayed they wouldn't set bail for Nico, and I needed to hear firsthand.

I arrived at the downtown Brooklyn courthouse early that morning. Once I found the courtroom where Nico's hearing would be held, I took a seat in the back. It was hot as shit in the building. It was the middle of winter and cold as hell outside, but they had it blasting to the point I was getting dizzy. I took off my coat and wanted to take off my hat, but I didn't want to be seen, especially by Nico.

More and more people started coming in filling up the wooden benches, then one particular person caught my eye. She strutted to the front of the courtroom and took a seat behind the defense table. Even to court, that chicken head bitch Porscha didn't know how to represent. She had on some low-cut red dress that was made so cheaply that if you pulled one piece of thread, the whole ensemble would fall apart. I so badly wanted to jump across these benches and finish where I left off, but I had to remind myself I was keeping a low profile. Seeing Porscha confirmed that Nico was getting exactly what he deserved. He was still seeing that bitch after he swore he was done with her. Niggas weren't shit.

Finally at a quarter to ten they brought Nico out. When they called his name, Porscha sat up extra straight and smiled at him like she was his wife. *Yeah bitch, you can do that bid wit' him too like you his wife,* I thought to myself.

When the Judge called his name, Nico stood next to his high-profile Jewish attorney, looking prouder than ever, even in his orange jumpsuit.

The prosecutor argued that bail shouldn't be set for Nico, not only because of the heinous nature of the crime, but because it was also a double homicide. He also stated that Nico was a flight risk, and due to his illegal drug activity, was a menace to society.

Nico's attorney argued that Nico was an upstanding businessman in the community and that he acted in self defense.

They went back and forth, and finally the judge sided with the prosecution and denied bail.

Nico's attorney immediately demanded that his client wanted a speedy trial.

Once the judge gave his ruling, I quietly got up to leave when I heard someone say, "Precious, is that you?" I tried to step up my speed, but then they got louder. "Precious Cummings, is that you?" I turned to see who had blown my cover, and instantly Nico and I made eye contact. If looks could kill I would've died that morning in the downtown

Brooklyn courthouse. Nico stared at me until the bailiff took him away.

"Don't you remember me, Precious? I used to keep you sometimes when your mother had to work."

"Yes," I said, nodding my head and wanting to punch the older lady in her mouth. "Hi, Ms. Duncan. How are you?"

"I'm good. I haven't seen you since you were a little girl. You have grown up to be so beautiful."

"Thank you," I said, trying to edge myself out the door.

"I hope you not in no trouble, being down here in the courthouse and all."

I wanted to be like, "I can ask you the same question," but I didn't want to start a scene. "No, I was just checking up on a friend of mine. I really have to be going. I'll tell my mother I saw you."

"You do that now."

Breathing a sigh of relief to finally be leaving the inferno, Porscha scandalous ass stopped me.

"What do you want?"

"I want to know why you came down here. You know Nico don't want to see you."

"Why is that?" I asked, wondering if he confided in her about my involvement with Ritchie.

"You know why."

Yeah, I did, but she obviously didn't or she would have been humming like the bird she was. "Listen, I'm not gonna discuss my relationship wit' my fiancée with you." I held up my engagement finger that still had the massive rock that Nico laced me with. "Whateva you got going on wit' him is cool 'cause you ain't nothing but a broke down, haggard, bootleg version of what I'll neva be. So keep it moving in that ten dollar, which includes the cost of those patent leather shoes you rockin' ensemble, and step the fuck off before I wax that ass one more time."

"Ain't nobody stuttin' you, Precious. You a dead bitch. You a dead bitch," she repeated.

My natural reflex kicked in and I balled up my fist ready to Mike Tyson her ass, when a security guard who had been watching our argument unfold, stepped in and grabbed my arm mid-air. "Miss, calm down," the officer said, now holding both my arms gently.

"Nah, let her go. I wish you would put yo' hands on me, Precious!" Porscha raged, trying to egg me on.

"I'm going to ask you to leave this area now, before I cite you for disruption," he said as Porscha rolled her eyes and walked away.

I was breathing so hard. I felt like that bitch was threatening my life. I was consumed with anger.

"Listen, you seem like a nice young lady so please calm down and leave without having another altercation with that woman. She's not worth it. Next time I might not be there to stop you, and it could be you in front of that judge."

I nodded my head, knowing what the security guard said was true. I got my bearings together and left.

Since I was in Brooklyn, I took a ride over to my moms' apartment to see how she was doing. When I unlocked the door, I immediately closed it and looked at the apartment number to make sure I was at the right place. I opened the door back up and was bugging at how clean the place was.

The walls were newly painted, the hardwood floors were in perfect condition and the whole apartment had new furniture. It didn't even look like the same place. I opened the refrigerator and not a bottle of liquor was in sight. Nothing but juice, water, fruit and other healthy foods, which made me wonder if my moms had died and someone else took over her apartment.

"Precious, I wasn't expecting to see you today, but I'm glad you're here," I heard my moms say.

When I turned towards the door to answer her, my heart almost stopped. I stood speechless.

"Precious, are you OK?" my moms said repeatedly as she stroked my hair.

"What happened to you?"

"I took your advice and got myself together. The last time you were here, I decided to quit using cold turkey. I truly felt ashamed that day, Precious."

I couldn't get over how beautiful my moms looked. She picked up weight and her hourglass shape was still intact. Her skin was glowing and her sandy brown hair was cut short and streaked with blonde highlights. It made her green eyes stand out even more. All the beauty that was hidden because of the drugs was now coming through. It was amazing. I just hugged her and wouldn't let go. For the first time in my life I had a mother.

For the rest of the day we sat down and talked to each other like human beings for the first time. Every word I said was brand new to my moms because she was hearing it with a clear mind, not one that was consumed with drugs. The six hours I spent with my mother were the happiest moments of my life.

"Momma, I have to meet with a friend of mine, but I'ma come back over when I'm done. You really look incredible. I'm so proud of you."

"Thank you. You be careful. I love you, Precious."

"I love you too."

My life finally had meaning. I decided that when I bought my house, I was bringing my mother with me. We could both leave Brooklyn and start over together. Maybe even open up a beauty salon or a nail shop together. We would be the flyest mother and daughter team ever.

Getting caught up in the future I was now planning, I looked at my watch and realized I only had an hour before I was supposed to meet up with Boogie. I needed to go all the way back to my storage spot in Jersey to get the cash I had to hit him off with. There was no way I was going to make it there and back in an hour, so I called Boogie and told him I would be an hour late. Luckily traffic wasn't that bad and I was making good time.

As I was coming back over the bridge, Inga's named popped up on my cell. I figured Porscha must've told Tanisha's cousin about our episode at the courthouse this morning and Inga was calling to get the dirt from me. "Hello."

"What up, Precious?"

"Nothing. Just handling some things. I'm kinda busy. What's up?"

"Oh, nothing. Where you at?"

"In the streets."

"Oh, you in Brooklyn?"

"Nah, that's not what I said. I'm in the streets," I replied, feeling funny about how Inga was coming at me.

"So when you coming back over to Brooklyn, 'cause I wanted to see you?"

"I'm not sure. You haven't been staying at my place in Harlem."

"No. Wit' the pregnancy and all, my moms wanted me to be close by family."

"That's cool."

"Do you want to stop by and pick up your apartment keys since I won't be staying there?"

"I'm good. I have an extra set. Inga, I hate to cut this short, but like I said, I'm in the middle of handling some things. We'll get up later." That nauseated feeling was coming over me but I tried to shake it off as just being overwhelmed by seeing Nico and my encounter with Porscha.

When I pulled up to Boogie's shop it was almost eight o'clock. I parked around the back so nobody could see my car from the main road.

"What up, ghetto queen?" Boogie smiled and said when I walked in the door. I knew it was because of the 100 grand I agreed to pay him for having his people set all my shit up so my money would be clean.

"I know I'm late, but I hope yo' people still coming," I said, feeling anxious.

"No doubt. I got you covered. You got that money for me?"

"Of course. It's in the car. After we finish up I'll give it to you."

"Look at you, Precious, being all business-minded. You've come a long way."

I was looking out the window blinds, patiently wait-ing for Boogie's people to show up. "Who the peoples you dealing wit' on this anyway?"

"Oh, these my folks. They fuck with a cat who deal with a lot of major hustlers out here, getting they shit in order. When I told them it was a female looking to clean up a mil-lion dollars, they damn near had a heart attack."

"You told them my name?"

"Yeah, but they family. They know old school rules. They just wanted to make sure you weren't the police or nothing. It's not every day a woman comes through with that type of money to wash."

"So, what's the dude's name?"

"Who? My nephews'?"

"No, the dude yo' nephews fuck wit."

"Oh, I think they said his name is Tommy?"

Before I could vomit, I saw Tommy's truck pulling up in front of the shop. "Oh shit, Boogie."

"What's wrong, Precious."

"Boogie, this is a trap. Shit, fuck!"

"Stop tripping. I told you them my nephews."

"Boogie, Tommy used to work for Nico. I saw him leaving our crib yesterday. He came there looking for the money." My hands were shaking as I ran to the door to lock it.

"Precious, you sure it's the same Tommy?"

"Yes, that's his truck outside right now. Come on, Boogie, let's go out the back. I parked my car out there. We can duck these motherfuckers before they get inside."

But before we could take another step, the front door glass flew everywhere from the bullets that Tommy sprayed. Boogie and I both threw our bodies down on the floor.

"Get the fuck up!" Tommy yelled as he and two other guys entered the shop.

"Where the fuck is the million dollars, Precious?"

Boogie stood up before I did and recognized the two other men as his nephews. "Lamont, Andre, what ya doing? You got yo' friend fucking up my shop. What is this all about?"

"Listen, Boogie," the taller, darker nephew said. "We

ain't got no beef wit' you, but this a million dollars we talking 'bout. The three of us gonna split that shit."

"Lamont Johnson, I know you ain't telling me you sold me out."

"Boogie, chill. You already chipped. Just have shorty hand over that money and we can all walk away from this wit' no problem."

"You sonofabitch!" Boogie yelled, leaping towards his nephews.

"Pops, you betta chill," Tommy warned as he raised his gun to Boogie's chest. Through all this I was still on the floor trying to figure out a way out of this bullshit.

"Precious, get the fuck up."

I slowly stood, locking eyes with Tommy.

"I know you didn't think I was gonna let you keep that money. Soon as I heard Nico was locked up and Ritchie was dead, I started thinking about getting hold of that money. I had to find out certain facts before I knew that the deal neva went down so the money had to still be in the house where I dropped it off. But yo' slick ass had already swooped it up by the time I got there. You taking it neva crossed my mind. I figured once the streets got word that Nico Carter was locked up, some gutsy nigga broke in his crib trying to clean him out and came across all that loot. It wasn't until my boy, Lamont here told me about a friend his uncle was helping out who had a million dollars, did it all start coming together."

"How you gonna steal from Nico? He was good to you, Tommy."

"Fuck Nico. He didn't give a damn about nobody but himself. He was living the high life while the rest of us out there busting our asses. Nico can fucking rot in that jail cell for all I care. Enough talk about that shit. Where's the money before I start dropping bodies up in here?"

"You ain't dropping shit, you punk-ass nigga. Now get the fuck out my shop before ya start something that you won't be able to finish."

"Old man, shut the fuck up," Tommy barked.

"Yeah, Boogie, shut the fuck up before we have to show you what's up," the once silent nephew, Andre echoed.

"Boy, I'ma whip yo' ass," Boogie trilled, raising his hand to back smack his nephew as a reminder to respect your elders. But that lesson would not be learned. Without warning, Andre blasted off his gun, shooting Boogie twice, once in the chest and last in the face. Boogie's brains splattered on the wall and a few drops of blood even landed on my cheek. I put my hands over my mouth, horrified by what I witnessed. I knew that I would be next. They would never let me leave alive. I was an eyewitness to a murder.

"Why you do that?" Lamont said to Andre.

"It was reflex. He was about to slap me like I was a bitch."

"Fuck all that. We need to hurry up. Precious, where the money at?"

"In my car."

"A'ight, move. Let's go get it," Tommy directed. "Yah go pull the truck around to the back while I go get this money."

"We gon' clean out the register first," Lamont said.

"Nigga, we about to split a million dollars and you talking about cleaning out the cash register. What is you smoking? We need to get the fuck up outta here. Somebody could've heard the gunshots and called the police."

"You right. We gon' pull the car around." Tommy tossed Lamont his keys and escorted me out the back. My feet moved slowly trying to buy myself time to come up with a plan. I looked straight ahead as Tommy kept his Berretta pointed to my back. I could feel him sizing me up as he smacked his lips and whistled in his attempt to taunt me.

"Damn, Precious, it's too bad shit had to end this way. You a bad bitch. I wish I could make you my girl. But if Nico ever heard about that, he would put a hit out on me from his jail cell," Tommy said with a chuckle.

"What do you think he's gonna do when he finds out you robbed me to get his money?"

"How is he gonna ever know?" That was a clear indication that he had no plans to let me live. "I wish I had more time. I would love to get up in that pussy," Tommy added, furthering the insult.

When we got to my car I popped the trunk. Tommy lifted it and saw a bunch of bags stacked on top of each other. "Which bag has the money?"

"The black one."

"All these bags are black. You dig through this shit. Them goofy niggas still ain't pulled the truck around, and I'm damn sure not about to let you make a run for it while I'm rummaging through these bags. So hurry up and get my money."

Tommy eyed me like a hawk as I pretended to look for the money. The million dollars wasn't even in the car. The only money I had was the $100,000 I brought for Boogie, and that was in the front seat. I was fidgeting around in the trunk for my savior, and when I found it I cocked my 9mm right before I tossed one of the black bags in Tommy's face. He lost his balance and the gun he was holding fell out of his hand. I used the opportunity to blast Tommy three times in the head before he even knew what hit him. I slammed the trunk and jumped in my car.

The treacherous nephews pulled up right when I was taking off. They saw Tommy splashed out on the cement and rolled right over him in their quest to get to me. Lamont was driving and Andre was busting off as we flew down Flatbush Avenue. They were gaining on me, so I pressed down on the accelerator, swerving trying not to hit anybody. Two more bullets hit my car and Lamont was pulling up so Andre would be directly on my side.

The light ahead was about to turn red and I noticed a truck about to pull out from the right side of the street. When the light turned green and the truck started pulling off, I jammed my foot on the gas and swiftly cut across the car Lamont was driving and cut in front of the truck, barely sliding through. By the time Lamont realized what I was doing, he couldn't hit his brakes fast enough and he collided into the side of the truck. The entire car exploded into flames instantly.

I drove off once again beating death.

Friend or Foe

Watching Lamont and Andre die in the car explosion had me shook up. I pulled over to side of the street, as everyone watched from a distance the horrific scene that was straight out a movie flick. I was in no condition to drive to Jersey, so I headed to my mother's crib. I kept switching the radio off and on in an attempt to get my mind off everything that happened in the last couple of hours. I couldn't believe Boogie was dead and his own nephew killed him.

The street life had no loyalty to no one, not even family. Being up close as Boogie's brains were splashed everywhere was making my body weak. The dried up blood was still resting on my face. I had no tissue, so I tried to use my hands to scrub the blood off, but it only made my face red and bruised. This was a nightmare, and I couldn't imagine it getting any worse.

When I drove up to the projects, I sat in my car for a few minutes, getting my thoughts together. I knew my mother would immediately sense something was terribly wrong, but I wasn't ready to tell her all the grimy details of what had taken place in my life. She'd finally gotten her life together and I didn't want her stressing over my problems. Before I got out the car I fixed my hair and spit on my hands to wipe off the dried blood on my face. I was determined to appear as if everything was straight when my mother saw me.

I took a deep breath when I opened the apartment door. It was pitch black, which was unusual. My mother never went to bed before one o'clock and she always fell asleep on the living room couch with the television on.

I finally located the light switch and to my despair the entire place had been ransacked. The brand new couch my mother purchased was cut up. The kitchen cabinets were open with broken dishes everywhere. The plants that were in the window were now knocked on the floor with dirt all over. I slowly walked towards the hallway and saw the words *"You're A Dead Bitch,"* written on the walls.

My whole body became flooded with the most agonizing twinge I ever experienced. At that moment, I knew my life would never be the same.

I didn't even want to walk in my mother's room because reality would truly set in. Her door was slightly ajar. When I pushed it completely open, I saw my beautiful mother's body lying there on the bed with her head completely severed. My knees completely buckled and I fell to the floor. For the first time, since I was a little girl, I cried. The tears flowed, and they wouldn't stop.

It was as if all the heartache and pain from so many years roared out begging to be released. I not only cried for myself, but I cried for my mother, the mother that I just found only earlier today. Now she'd been taken away from me, before I could enjoy all the moments that I dreamed of all my life. Dreams that I never believed could be possible and now they wouldn't be. The shimmer of hope my mother gave me when I looked into her beautiful green eyes today had died with her.

On my way back to Jersey, I contemplated ending my life, by driving off the side of the road. The only thing that stopped me was that I didn't have the guts. With all the bullshit I'd seen and done, I was scared to end it all. I was riddled with guilt. My revenge on Nico caused the death of Boogie and my mother. I would never be able to live that down.

When I made it back to the hotel room, I raided the mini bar and guzzled down every ounce of alcohol available. All I wanted was to sleep without enduring the pain.

"Oh goodness," I mumbled out loud when the ringing of my cell phone wouldn't stop. "What?"

"Precious, wake up," I heard Inga yelling through the phone.

"I'm up. What is it?"

"Precious, I have something to tell you." There was silence on the phone for a few seconds. "Precious are you there?"

"Yeah, what do you have to tell me?"

"It's about your mother and Boogie."

"What about them?" I asked, not wanting Inga to have a clue I already knew.

"They're dead, Precious. Both of them were murdered sometime last night."

"Damn, do they have any idea who did it or why?"

"Well, Boogie was found dead inside his shop and Tommy, that kid that worked for Nico, was found killed right outside the shop. The cops tryn' to piece all the shit together."

"What about my mother?"

"They don't know. Because of the profession she was in, they thinking it could've been anybody."

"My mother had cleaned her life up. She wasn't in that

profession no more, so tell them bitch-ass cops and any-body else that's running they mouth to shut the fuck up. They don't know nothing about my mother. She better than all of them!" I screamed, as I tried to defend my mother in death, since she was never defended in life.

"Precious, I'm sorry. I had no idea yo' moms turned her life around."

"How would you know?" I responded sarcastically.

"So when you coming back to Brooklyn?"

"Inga, I don't fucking know. Maybe neva. Coming through BK seems like a death sentence to me. Five moth-erfuckers I know have died in the last week. I don't want no parts of Brooklyn right now."

"So where you gon' go?"

"Why the fuck you keep asking me so many damn ques-tions? You been coming at me like you the feds since you called me about Nico's arrest."

"Damn, Precious, you my best friend I'm just worried about you. Excuse me."

"You got enough to worry about. You need to concentrate on that seed you got growing inside you instead of wondering when the next time I'm stopping through Brooklyn."

"You know what, Precious? I know emotionally you fucked up in the game right now. First, Nico get locked up and now both your mom and Boogie get killed. That's a lot to swallow, so I'm not gonna take none of the shit you say-ing personally. Just know I'm here for you."

"Yeah, I hear you, Inga. I'll speak to you later."

My head was killing me and the conversation I had with Inga didn't help. I had to get my mind off all the bullshit. I dragged myself out of bed, took a shower and headed to

Short Hills Mall. Shopping would at least numb my mind momentarily.

After racking up clothes from Fendi, Gucci, Versace and just about every other store in the mall, I went to the nail salon for a pedicure. I was reading my *XXL* magazine when I heard the girl sitting next to me complaining about how her roommate bolted on her without notice, and she didn't know how she would be able to maintain her rent. I instantly thought about how it was time for me to get the hell out of that hotel and this might be the perfect opportunity.

Before getting too excited, on the sly I sized the girl up. She reminded me of one of those college prep girl types, all goody-goody and shit. Which was cool since I needed a major break from my normal 'bout-it, 'bout-it chicks. When the girl got off the phone I decided to put on my best All American girl voice and inquire about her apartment.

"Hi, I didn't mean to eavesdrop on your conversation, but I heard you say something about needing a roommate." I then peeped the girl doing her own sizing up of me. She first eyed my snakeskin Gucci purse and scanned down to my matching boots. Her eyes finally landed on the few pieces of ice I was rockin'.

"Yeah, my girlfriend just broke out on me without any notice. She got some new boyfriend and moved in with him. There is no way I can afford the rent on my own. Are you looking for a place to live?"

"Actually, I am. I just moved here from Philly and I'm staying at a hotel. I was going to start looking for my own place, but it would be great to have a roommate, especially since I don't know anybody here."

"What hotel are you staying at?"

"The Hyatt Regency in Jersey City."

"Oh, I know where that is. It's nice."

"Yeah, but you can't stay in a hotel forever."

"True. Well I live in Edgewater. My rent is a little expensive because I live on River Road-they actually call it Rappers Row."

"Why's that?"

"Because a lot of Rappers and industry people live in the condos and high rises on that street."

"Oh that's cool. So how much is the rent?"

"Three thousand a month, so if you took the place your part would be fifteen hundred plus half for utilities. Is that within your budget?"

"Definitely. I could even pay you six months upfront so you don't have to be worried about me leaving you in a bad predicament like your other roommate did." The girls eyes lit up and I knew it would work out. Money had a way of doing that to people.

"Cool. You'll love the place. The building is fabulous and everyone is really friendly. Your room is a nice size and you have your own bathroom."

"Are you saying the place is mine?"

"I guess so, if you want it. You can come take a look today, and if you like it you can move in immediately. Oh my goodness I'm about to have a new roommate and I don't even know your name." We both laughed.

"I'm Precious." I extended my hand. "It's nice to meet you."

"Rhonda, and it's nice to meet you, too."

After finishing up our pedicures and letting the polish dry, I followed Rhonda to her apartment. She lived in a beautiful complex called Independence Harbor. The small city was different than any place I had ever been. It seemed so bright and cheerful, nothing like the projects in Brooklyn. The apartment was spacious, and the huge windows had beautiful views of New York City and the Hudson River.

"I want it."

"Great. I'll write up an agreement between us, for your protection and mine."

"That's fine."

"You're also welcome to use the furniture that my friend left behind."

"Thanks for the offer, but I'll get my own."

"Okay, so when are you going to move in?" Rhonda asked, sounding extremely excited.

"Is tomorrow too soon?"

"No, that's fine."

"I'm going to get my stuff from the hotel and then start doing some furniture shopping for my bedroom."

"Precious, I have a great feeling about this."

"Me, too, Rhonda."

When I left my new roommate I did have a great feeling. Although only a tunnel and a bridge separated us, I felt like Brooklyn was thousands of miles away. Before I went back to the hotel, I stopped by my storage unit to pick up all my clothes, shoes and other belongings. The only thing I left was my money. The next morning I checked out my hotel room and headed to my new apartment.

When I arrived Rhonda had our agreement already prepared. I handed her the $9000 in cash and the biggest smile crossed her face.

"Precious, I hope you don't mind me asking, but what

do you do? All your belongings are like top designer stuff. You're driving a new Benz, and your jewelry is really nice. Then you give me $9000 upfront. Money obviously isn't an issue for you."

In my mind I debated for a second if I wanted to tell Rhonda the truth. I was getting tired of talking all proper and tying to pretend to be so happy-go-lucky.

"My ex-man was a kingpin. He's the one that bought me all this stuff. Before he got locked up, he left me a nice lump of money. I'm what you call a hustler's girl."

"Wow. He must have been some hustler."

"No doubt."

"So what is he locked up for?"

"Murder."

"Who did he kill?"

"His best friend." Rhonda stood there, shaking her head. Her expression was that of surprise. She definitely didn't know anything about the streets.

"My life is awfully boring compared to the one you've seemed to live."

She had no idea, I said to myself.

"Enough about me, what do you do?"

"I work at Atomic Records in the marketing department."

"That's dope. So you must know mad celebrities?"

"Yeah, but after awhile they become just regular people who are a lot more demanding and anal."

"That's believable. They probably so used to motherfuckers kissing they ass, they start acting real simple."

"Basically," Rhonda said in agreement. "So are you going to look for a job? But then you probably don't need the money."

"I just graduated from high school a year ago. I was actually thinking about maybe going to college or some type of school. I think I do need to be more productive with my time."

"Speaking of time, I need to get to work. Make yourself at home. Here's your key to the apartment and I wrote down my cell phone number and left it on the refrigerator. If you need anything, don't hesitate to call me."

"Thanks, Rhonda. You mad cool."

For the next few weeks, I got settled in my new place. I got rid of all the garbage that was in my bedroom and hooked it up with some fly-ass furniture I got from this place called Moda Furniture. Between decorating my new room and hanging out with Rhonda I watched the news and read the newspaper.

Because Nico's attorney requested a speedy trial, he would be going to court in the next couple of weeks. The high profile case was drawing all sorts of different opinions from legal experts. Some said he would be found guilty and many others said the Prosecution's case was weak and Nico would walk. All I thought was *Say It Ain't So*. There was no way Nico could beat the case. If he did, there would be no place on this earth I could hide. He would hunt me down like an animal.

I was already scared as it was; so scared that I didn't even want to attend my mother's funeral. I tracked down the lady, Ms. Duncan, that I ran into at the courthouse that day, and called her. She had heard about my mother's death and was actually devastated. She was one of the few people that remembered how beautiful and special my mother was at one time in her life.

I told her I was going through some things, but wanted my mother to have a beautiful funeral and tombstone. I met up with her in the city and gave her thirty thousand dollars to handle all the arrangements and to keep something for all her help. The day of the funeral I watched from a distance, not knowing if my enemies were tracking me. To my surprise, a lot of people showed up to pay their last respects to my mother. I couldn't help but think that it was a shame how people would celebrate you in death instead of when you are still alive to see it.

"How much?" I asked the cashier, while putting my groceries in the cart. I seemed to live at Pathmark. In Brooklyn I ate out just about every day and night. I was constantly running the streets, so I never had time for a home-cooked meal. But since I didn't know nobody in Jersey, I was always in the crib and whipping up meals was becoming a hobby. As I handed the cashier the money, I faintly heard the sounds of my cell ringing. My purse was lodged between the bags and I barely caught the call. "Hello," I said, sounding frazzled.

"Precious, I need to see you."

"Inga?" The number came up private and the voice sounded serious, so I wasn't positive if it was her or not.

"Yeah, it's me. We need to talk."

"About what?" I hadn't spoken to Inga in almost three months so her funky tone was rubbing me the wrong way.

"We can discuss that when I see you."

"No, we can discuss it right now, or you won't be seeing me."

"I don't want to do this over the phone, Precious. I need to see you face to face."

"On the real, Inga, I'm not feeling your funky attitude. I'm also not feeling meeting you somewhere 'cause how you coming at me make me think this might be some sort of set up. And if that's the case, you need to step the fuck back 'cause I would hate to have to bust off on yo' sneaky ass."

"Ain't nobody tryna set you up, Precious. No matter what, we still peoples. But I do need to speak to you, but I would prefer to do it in person."

"When?"

"Today, if possible."

"A'ight, meet me in the city in an hour. I'll call and let you know the exact location when I get there. And, Inga, don't try no slick shit."

I rushed home, put my groceries away and hopped in the shower. I got dressed quickly and then headed over to my storage spot to pick up my gun. As far as I was concerned, me and Inga were no longer peoples, and I didn't trust her. When I met up with her, if I got so much as a hint she was up to no good, I was gonna waste her ass, pregnant or not.

When I got to the city, I called Inga on her cell and told her to meet me in Union Square in twenty minutes. I was already parked on the corner, but it would give me an opportunity to observe and see if I saw anybody that looked suspicious.

Inga finally showed up, with belly poked out before her. I watched her for ten more minutes, seeing if she got on the phone with anybody or if she was making any eye contact with the people in the crowds. Once I felt safe, I grabbed my purse with the gun safely inside and walked up behind her.

"What's up, Inga?"

"Oh shit, you scared the fuck outta me, Precious."

"That was the point," I said, walking towards the bench. "Come on let's have a seat over here. So what's up?"

Inga took a deep breath before beginning.

"Precious, I want you to be honest wit' me about something."

"OK."

"Precious, were you seeing Ritchie behind my back?"

"Who told you that?"

"That don't matter."

"If you want me to answer your question it do."

"Porscha said that Nico told her that you were a snake bitch because you were fucking his best friend behind his back. He also said you was pregnant by Ritchie and was planning on leaving him so ya could be together."

"Oh, so you talk to Porscha now? Ya'll friends."

"That's not even the point, Precious. I want to know if what Nico said is true."

"No, it is the point if you fucking wit' my enemy."

"Are you gonna answer me or not?"

"I'll tell you the truth. Yeah, I was fucking Ritchie, but no, I wasn't pregnant by him, although I told Nico I was."

"But, Precious, why?" Inga asked with pain in her voice.

"Because after I found out about Porscha, I wanted Nico to pay, and I knew fucking his best friend would do the trick."

"But, you knew Ritchie was my boyfriend, and we cared about each other."

"Inga, wake up! Ritchie didn't give a fuck about you. He used you to make me jealous. He begged me to leave Nico.

"I told you not to get caught up in that nigga, but you swore he was the one. I did you a favor by getting him out yo' life, but then you wanna fuck around and have a baby for this dude."

I sat shaking my head. Inga was stunned by what I said, but she asked for the truth. "Inga, I didn't mean for you to get hurt, but Nico had to pay. Ritchie won't no good. He didn't think twice about crossing Nico. You shouldn't take any of this so personally. Ritchie didn't mean nothing to me. He was a means to an end."

"Nico didn't kill Ritchie because he found out he was setting him up. He killed him because you told him that you were fucking Ritchie," Inga said as if all the pieces were coming together. "That's what happened isn't it?"

"Why don't you ask Porscha, since she's your new yellow pages."

"I don't need to. You planned all of this. You knew Nico would kill Ritchie once he found out, and you made sure he did. You knew I was pregnant, Precious. How could you have my baby's daddy set up to be killed?"

"Inga, Ritchie didn't even want that baby. You told me yourself he said he would cut the baby out of you if you didn't have an abortion. Bitch, I'm the one that hit you off wit' 50 G's so yo' broke ass could give yo' baby a start in life. That's more than Ritchie ever did for you, or would've done. So don't sit up here, tryna blame me for getting knocked up by a man that didn't want you or his seed."

"Things might've been different if you would've stayed out of our relationship. He didn't start changing until he started fucking you. Now Ritchie is dead, and my child will neva know his father."

"Well, bitch, join the motherfucking club 'cause I don't know my daddy neither, and what." Inga turned her face away.

I didn't know if it was because of what I said or because

of the afternoon sun glaring in our path. The wind was blowing the trees in all directions as adults and children relishing in the beautiful spring day strolled past us. By the idyllic picture, the strangers going by would've never expected that two former best friends were having a life-changing conversation.

"Was it all worth it, just so you could punish Nico for cheating on you wit' some trick?"

"Believe it or not, I've asked myself the same question and the answer is yes. He disrespected me to the fullest, knowing that the streets be watching. If I had done the same thing to him, he would've sent me home in a body bag."

"Have you ever thought that he still might?"

"Not behind bars, he won't."

"Well, for your sake you betta pray that's where he stays. Because if Nico gets out, he won't rest until you six feet under." Inga wasn't telling me nothing that I didn't already know. Nico getting out could never be. It was no longer safe for both of us to walk the same streets.

Baller Bitch

The headline on the front cover of the *"New York Post"* read 'Notorious Kingpin Found Guilty of Murder'. Underneath there was a big picture of Nico handcuffed being escorted out the courtroom. Unlike the first time I saw him in court, his ensemble didn't consist of an orange jumpsuit. He was in one of his custom-made designer suits, looking more like a Wall Street business man than a cold-blooded killer. I was finally able to exhale, knowing that Nico would be spending the rest of his life behind bars. After reading the inside story, I went to celebrate by cooking a big breakfast.

"Good morning, Precious," Rhonda said when I entered the kitchen.

"Good morning," I said sounding unusually chipper for this early in the morning.

"Anything good in the paper?" Rhonda asked as she picked up the paper I just put down on the counter.

"What's this?" she said, reading the headlines about Nico. "Look at him he's a hottie. Who would think someone that fine could be a murderer? Now I know where all the good looking men are-locked up."

I refused to put my two cents in the conversation because I didn't want Rhonda to know that my kingpin and the one on the cover of the Post were one in the same. "Do you have any plans tonight?" she asked, finally putting the paper down.

"No, I'm chilling."

"Well, I don't know if you feel like it, but we're having an album release party for Supreme. You're welcome to come."

"Supreme the rapper?"

"Yeah. He's a cutie right?"

"I didn't know Supreme is on the same label you work for. His music is slick. But, nah, I'm not going out tonight. But you can bring me back his new CD."

"Why don't you want to come? It'll be fun."

"I just wanna stay at home tonight, stuff my face and watch my favorite DVD, *"Paid in Full."*

"Alright. Well, don't wait up for me. I won't be home until late."

"Cool, don't shake yo' ass too hard," I said smiling. Part of me did want to go to the party, but the other part of me wanted to just chill.

I'd been feeling especially uneasy after my conversation with Inga in Union Square. Hearing her say Nico would hunt me down and kill me if he beat his case made my blood run cold. For the last few weeks I'd been on pins and needles, waiting for the trial to end and the verdict to be announced. But even hearing guilty, I wasn't completely stress free. For the rest of the day I pretty much moped around, doing entirely too much thinking, until my cell phone rang. I hated answering private calls, but I was happy to do anything to get my mind off Nico. "Hello."

"Precious, what's up? You got a minute?" I immediately recognized Inga's voice and everything inside of me wanted to hang up the phone on her. We hadn't spoken to each other since our meeting in the city, and I had no interest in speaking to her. When she revealed that her and Porscha were now talking, which in my mind meant trading information, I didn't want nothing to do with Inga.

"Yeah, I got a minute, and that's about it."

"Well, then let me get right to it. I need some money." I had to step back from my phone to make sure I heard Inga correctly.

"Excuse me. Did I hear you correctly?"

"Yes. You were the only person I knew to call for help."

"Before I even respond, what happened to the fifty G's I gave you less than six months ago?"

"It's gone. I had to buy a car and to get some things for me and the baby."

"Inga, the baby ain't even here yet and you spent all the money. What type of car did you buy?"

"That don't matter, Precious, the point is, I don't have no more, and the baby will be here in a couple of months. So I was hoping you could hit me off wit' a hundred thousand."

"I don't have a hundred thousand, and even if I did, I wouldn't give it to yo' simple ass."

"You ain't gotta call me no names, neither. I just figured since you stole that million from Nico, the least you could do was put a hundred thousand in my pocket, since you are responsible for making my unborn child fatherless." With that said I was tempted to break the promise I made to myself of staying out of Brooklyn so I could go whip Inga's ass.

"I don't know what kind of slick shit you tryna pop, but I didn't steal no million dollars from Nico. I'm tryna maintain out in these streets just like you. So whateva you heard or you think you know is all bullshit. As for your bastard child being fatherless, you gonna have to take the charge on that for being a stupid bitch."

"Precious, you always thought you were hot shit and you still do. You walk these streets not thinking about nobody but yourself. But bitch, you can't hide forever.

"You think you can break outta Brooklyn and leave everybody behind and forget about all the havoc you caused. You the reason Ritchie is dead, you the reason that Nico is locked up and my instincts tell me you responsible for Boogie and your moms, death too. But all your scheming is going to come back on you and you gon' take it in blood."

"Fuck you, Inga!" I bellowed before throwing my cell across the room where it shattered against the wall. I was getting closer to going over the edge. I immediately threw on my clothes, grabbed my purse and headed out the door.

As I hurried through the Mall toward the T-Mobile store to replace my cell phone, a cherry red halter dress hanging in a window caught my eye. It had a wood o-ring and asymmetric lattice hem. At that moment, I decided to go to the album release party tonight and shake my ass with Rhonda.

Never one to be on time, I arrived when the party was about to end. I had called Rhonda and told her I was on my way, and now two hours later, I was just getting to the front door of the club. There were a few people on the same time schedule as me who were also just arriving.

As I was walking in, a group of people rushed pass me to a waiting Suburban. I glanced to see who it was since there was a chaotic buzz surrounding them. In an intense second my eyes locked with a sexy looking dude.

"You need to come in, Miss. there are people waiting behind you," the humongous bouncer demanded and snapped me out of the love connection I had just made.

When I turned back around, the Suburban had driven off. *I guess it wasn't meant to be* I thought to myself.

"There you are," Rhonda said as she greeted me at the door. "That sure was a long I'm on my way, Precious."

"Sorry, girl, but time is neva on my side."

"It was time well spent," Rhonda said as she glanced over my outfit." "That dress is fierce."

"I know right, it was actually my motivation for coming out tonight. I saw it and had to rock it. I wish I would've gotten here earlier 'cause it seem like it was cute."

"Yeah, it was. All the A-list celebrities we invited showed up."

"Where's the guest of honor."

"You just missed him." *Damn, could the sexy ma'fuckah I made eye contact wit' been Supreme. There was something familiar about him. Nah, that couldn't of been that nigga,* I thought to myself. "Come over to my table and have a couple of drinks before the party is officially over.

Although Rhonda had invited me to a few industry parties, this was the first one I ever came to. It definitely wasn't like the clubs in Brooklyn. The people in here gave off this aura of being on some real phony Hollywood type-shit. For the hour I was there, Rhonda spent half that time giving fake-ass hugs and kisses to a few motherfuckers that she obviously didn't like.

Everybody's favorite departing line was "I'll call you, let's do lunch." With all that said, the music was off the hook, the club was hot and, for the most part, the people were fly.

For the next few weeks, Rhonda and I lived on the party scene. After that one night I'd become addicted. There was this raw energy that engulfed you running in those circles. Since I had money to blow, I kept bottles of Cristal flowing at every club we went to. Rhonda would constantly joke with me and say, "Who was your ex-man? Was he on some New Jack City, Nino Brown type shit?"

I would just laugh and pop the next bottle. Something about Rhonda was really cool, though. I digged her so much that I even paid for her to get a complete makeover, which included hair, makeup and a new wardrobe. Rhonda was a semi-cute girl, she reminded me of a book smart version of Brandy. After we finished her makeover, she turned into the R&B version. Rhonda was overwhelmed by my generosity and her appreciation numbed all the different emotions that were swimming through my body.

"Precious, Funk Master Flex's annual car show is coming up," Rhonda informed me while we were having dinner at Houston's. The Hawaiian steak I was devouring tasted so good that it took me a moment to even listen to what Rhonda was saying.

"Car show," I finally said, right before taking another bite.

"Yeah, he has it every year. This year it's going to be at the Convention Center in Atlantic City on June 25 and 26. I think we should go."

"That's next weekend. I'm down."

I'd never been to a car show before, and back when I worked at Boogie's car detailing shop, the niggas would come through to get they rides extra fly to show up at Flex's shit. Now I would be attending so I had to be on point. I had plenty of ice, but I went and purchased a few new pieces of bling to rock.

By accident, I found this Dominican spot called Hair

Guild and the beautician blew out my hair so it was bone straight but with just the right amount of bounce. I had a closet full of clothes that I hadn't worn yet, but I still had to get a couple of new outfits just in case I didn't like anything I had at home.

Truth be told, I was hoping to find me a dude at the car show. Not to be my man but to fuck. The last time I had some dick was when I fucked Nico the night he killed Ritchie. That was months ago, and I was horny as shit. Rhonda didn't have the same problem as me because she had a boyfriend named Amir. He was a corny nigga, but he seemed like he was putting it down.

I can remember a couple of occasions when I was shaken from my sleep by the sounds of Rhonda screaming his name. Sometimes that shit would get me so turned on, I would have to finger myself until I had an orgasm and then fall back to sleep. I was tired of pleasing myself. I needed some good dick.

I was the epitome of a straight baller bitch when we pulled up on the scene in my spankin' clean Benz. Instead of putting on one of my many over-the-top outfits, I kept it simple and let my body and accessories speak for me. I had on some fitting just right Apple Bottom jeans with a crisp white tank top and some open-toe stilettos. With my ears, neck and wrist dripping in diamonds it was enough said. All I heard was loud whispers of people trying to figure out who I was. I put an extra strut in my walk as I parlayed through the crowd. All eyes were on me and the bitches were all hating. I couldn't blame them, because if I wasn't me I would be hating, too.

"Precious, this place packed. Everybody up in here."

"Tell me about it, there are so many cuties I don't know where to start."

"I do," Rhonda said all bold.

"Girl, shut up. You got a man."

"So what? You think I'm letting all this go to waste on one man. Oh, please."

"Ain't this some shit. You get a makeover and you 'un turned into a hot-ass bitch. It was something in your eyes that always told me there was a hoe underneath there."

"You got that right. And I will forever be grateful to you, Precious, for helping me discover it." I looked at Rhonda sideways, not sure if I wanted to take credit for that. I knew what type of trouble you could get in by being a hot tamale. I hoped that Rhonda wouldn't make the mistake of biting off more than she could chew. "Stay right here, Precious, I see this guy that I've been dying to meet. I'll be back."

In that quick second, Rhonda left me standing alone, while she went and chased some dick. I couldn't be mad at her because technically I was on the same mission; she just beat me to the punch.

Dudes kept pimping past me and the closer they got, they would slow down and make eye contact to try to get a vibe if I was interested or not. I would smack my lips and roll my eyes so they would keep it moving. Then a pair of eyes met mine and a sense of familiarity came over me.

"Didn't I see you outside a club about a month ago?" the sexy ma'fuckah asked me as a few of his homeboys and a couple of bodyguards lingered beside him.

"Aren't you the rapper, Supreme?"

"Yeah, that's me," the mellow-toned MC replied. "Aren't you

the young lady that was going into the club as I was leaving?"

"Yeah, that was me. You remember that." I said, surprised that he did.

"Of course, I'd never forget a face as beautiful as yours."

Now I never considered myself to be no groupie bitch. Even with all the hustler's I fucked with, I just wrote that off as me liking niggas with heavy pockets. I've watched videos and flipped through magazines seeing all these rap stars and other celebrities, and yes, the curiosity of how they lived was always there. But it wasn't that deep for me because where I came from, I was the hood superstar. I represented for my borough the same way these so-called celebrities represented for they clique.

Their fan base just so happened to reach millions of people where mine only reached thousands. But the feeling of being on top was still the same. So when Supreme was standing in front of me saying how beautiful I was, I wasn't sure if my pussy was getting extra wet because he was a rap superstar or because he was a sexy ma'fuckah. Or maybe it was a combination of both.

"Why you tryna make me blush in front of all these people out here?"

"That wasn't my intention. What I wanted was for you to walk with me, talk with me and then, hopefully exchange numbers with me. But that might be asking too much. What do you think?"

"Truthfully, I want to leave with you, be with you and hopefully chill with you for a long time." Before I could hear his response Rhonda was back.

"What's up, Supreme?" she said giving him a hug.

"Just so you know, I work with her-that's it," he said not

wanting me to feel uncomfortable.

"Supreme, that's my roommate. You don't have to explain yourself."

"Word. You guys live together? Damn, Rhonda you never told me you had this at home," Supreme pointed to me with his hands in a display position as if he was a game show host."

"She came to your album release party, but I think you had already left."

"Yeah, we made eye contact on my way out. Then I was blessed to see her once again today. Damn, baby, I didn't even get your name yet."

"Precious."

"That name fits you perfectly. So are you going to walk with me or what?"

"That depends. Are you going to leave with me, be with me and chill with me?"

"You didn't even have to ask me that twice. I heard you the first time and the answer is no doubt."

With that I took Supreme's hand and spent the entire duration of the car show as his date. Instead of staying in the hotel room with Rhonda I stayed with him in his suite at the Borgata. The first night, after all of us, including Rhonda, went out for dinner and drinks, I was ready to catch up for the sex drought I had been on.

After taking a shower I laid in the bed next to Supreme ready to do all sorts of tricks with my tongue, but he stopped me before I even made it to the nipples on his chest. "Precious, I just want you to fall asleep in my arms."

"I can do that right after we fuck."

"Baby, I don't want to fuck you?"

"What you mean you don't want to fuck me? What is something wrong wit' me or something?" I asked, feeling embarrassed that the nigga was turning me down.

"Precious, look at me," he said grabbing my face.

"Physically, you're perfect. And I want you in every way. When we become intimate, I don't want us to fuck. I want us to make love. There is a big difference. Precious, I'm truly feeling you. I was connected to you in just that brief moment we locked eyes in front of the club.

"You're special and I want our relationship to be special. That means taking our time and getting to know one another. That means getting past the lust and learning to appreciate what's on the inside. Will you do that with me, Precious? Take our time so we can build something real?"

I stared into Supreme's dark mysterious eyes in total confusion. No man had ever asked to get to know me as a person before. When I was ready to get twisted out, so were they. Here was this rap star, that probably had more pussy tossed his way than the law deemed legal, telling me that he wanted us to wait and get to know each other better first. His request seemed so pure that it was frightening to me. I didn't know how to respond, so I snuggled my warm body underneath his arms and fell asleep.

One Love

When Rhonda and I got back from Atlantic City, I couldn't get Supreme off my mind. That nigga had me straight tripping. He didn't want no ass, just conversation. The funny thing was in those two days I spent with him, I never felt closer to any man in my life. With all the talking we did, I got past the initial physical attraction and took time out to know the man.

Supreme was successful in getting me to do that. But I also had to admit to myself that the thought of having genuine feelings for him was scaring me. It was too late for that, though. I'd spent the last hour lying in my bed, staring at a picture we took at the car show, just missing him.

That was a clear indication to me that the tables might've turned, and he might have me open. As I smiled at the thought, I heard my cell phone ringing, which made my smile even brighter. I knew it had to be Supreme because after my last conversation with Inga, I had that phone cut off and got a new number. The only person that had it so far was Supreme. "Hi, baby," I said with that bubbly feeling in my stomach I heard you get when you catching feelings for somebody.

"Hi, baby to you, Precious, you been on my mind every second since I got up this morning. I need to see you."

"Tell me when 'cause I need to see you too."

"How 'bout I come get you after I finish up at the studio and we catch a bite to eat."

"What time do you think that'll be?"

"Eight or nine, is that cool?

"Definitely, I can't wait to see you." As much as I was looking forward to spending time with Supreme, I wanted him to put it down on me so freakin' bad. All this datin' and waitin' was about to make me go postal. I decided I would once again make the suggestion to him that we needed to cut all the foreplay, which in this case was all this dating and talking, and go straight to the dessert.

As it started getting closer to eight, I looked through my closet, wanting to pick out the right outfit. I didn't want it to scream "Please fuck me tonight," but the underlying meaning definitely had to be in effect.

"Precious are you home?" I heard Rhonda screaming while in the middle of trying on my eighth outfit.

"Yes," I answered walking towards the living room to get her opinion about my attire. I knew Supreme had me feeling some kinda way when I took to asking Rhonda for fashion advice. "How does this look on me?" I said, lacing up my corset top.

"Pretty damn good."

I looked up to see what the hell was going on with Rhonda's voice since the sound I heard was five octaves too low.

"Oh I'm sorry, Precious. This is Robert. I was seeing if you were home to let you know I had company. But he's right. The outfit is definitely hot," Rhonda said as she play-fully punched her friend on the arm for lusting after me in her face.

"Thanks, I guess I'll wear this."

"You must have a date with Supreme by the looks of you."

"Yes, as a matter of fact, I do."

"Well, have fun tonight, because I know I am." With that Rhonda grabbed Robert's hand and headed to her bedroom. This was the third guy Rhonda had over here in less than a week. She was going overboard. Not one to knock any woman for getting her shit off, but she was playing a dangerous game.

As far as her boyfriend Amir went, he assumed they were still a couple. But Rhonda seemed to have other ideas. I guess all those years of niggas not paying her no mind had caused her to lose her mind. She seemed to be on a mission to fuck every dude she ever had a crush on, which obviously was a lot. Never mind her though; she was getting enough dick for the both of us. It was time for me to get my own.

Admiring the view of the city from the deck of the Charter House restaurant, I said, "Supreme, I'm glad you took me here, this is crazy romantic."

"I knew you'd like it. I want to always keep things fresh and sexy with you."

"Yeah, that's what's up."

The nighttime breeze was making a tantalizing evening even more erotic. The gaze coming from Supreme's eyes made me hopeful that he had the same desire to get our fuck on tonight as me. "Precious, you are so beautiful. Who do you resemble, your mother or your father?" he asked, fucking up my whole sex fantasy that was just playing in my mind.

"I would have to say my mother," I quickly answered.

"I can't wait to meet her. The woman that gave birth to a daughter so gorgeous has to be special." Supreme wanting to meet my mother blew me away. No man had ever shown any sort of interest in wanting to meet a parent of mine. It was a damn shame that when one finally did, my mother was dead and gone.

"Unfortunately, Supreme, that'll neva happen."

"Why? are the two of you not on good terms?"

"We ain't on no terms. My mother is dead."

"What? Damn, baby, I'm sorry. How long has she been dead?"

"About six months."

"Wow, that's so recent." Supreme sat there for a minute shaking his head. "How did she die?"

I can't believe this nigga was making me relieve this shit all over again, I said to myself.

"My mother was murdered, Supreme, and before you come asking me 'bout my daddy, 'cause I know that's next, I don't know who he is," I shrieked. "I ain't neva met my daddy. My mother was a whore; she probably didn't know who my daddy was."

"Precious, I didn't mean to get you all upset. I shouldn't have came at you with all those questions."

"It's not your fault Supreme. How were you supposed to know that I came from nothing?"

"Precious, don't ever say that about yourself. You did come from something. You don't realize how special you are. But if you let me, I'll show you."

"I'd like that." For the next couple of hours Supreme and I just talked. True to form when he took me home, he gave me a kiss goodnight and kept it moving.

"How was your date with Supreme?" Rhonda asked, still up watching television.

"It was great, up to the point he dropped me off with a kiss and goodbye. Leaving me to once again go to bed finger fucking myself."

"You still haven't fucked him?"

"Hell no."

"Damn, Precious, I don't know how you're able to be around a guy as fine as Supreme and not get none."

"Who you telling? All this let's get to know each other first is so *'Leave it to Cleaver.'* It also doesn't help that I have to hear you climbing walls in the middle of the night."

"Don't get mad 'cause I'm getting some and you not."

"Where is your latest fuck toy anyway?"

"In the bed knocked out. Girl, I wore his ass out. We been fucking up a storm ever since you left."

Right before Rhonda was about to go into detail about her fuck fest, there was a knock at the door. "Who could that be this late?"

"Girl, that's probably Supreme. On his way home he had to turn around because he said fuck that. I need to get inside of Precious."

"You so crazy, you better go get the door before he changes his mind."

"You don't have to tell me twice, I said opening the door. Hi baby," Instead of Supreme, I was surprised to see Amir. "Amir, hi, I was expecting somebody else." I turned and looked over at Rhonda, knowing it was about to be some drama.

"That's alright. Is Rhonda here?" Amir asked, brushing past me before I could answer his question.

"Amir what you doing here?"

"I've been calling you all fucking night, but you turned your cell off and you haven't been answering your home phone. Where the fuck you been?"

"My battery on my cell died, and I just got back from going out to eat with Precious."

"Then why is Precious fully dressed and you got on your bathrobe?" *Amir appeared to be on the corny side but that nigga didn't miss a beat* I thought to myself as he immediately questioned Rhonda's story. Before she could come back with a lame ass excuse, Robert, wearing just his boxer shorts came walking out her bedroom, rubbing his eyes.

"Damn, Rhonda you fucked me so good, you almost put a nigga out for the night," Robert said before looking up and seeing Amir standing with the look of terror on his face. I put my head down, praying that Amir would be the bigger person and walk out the door. We all remained silent, waiting for Amir's reaction. No one in the room wanted to move first. Without warning, Amir balled up his fist and punched Rhonda in her face like she was a straight-up dude.

"Amir, stop!" she screamed between whacks.

"Robert, do something!" I shouted, but that punk-ass nigga stood there like a straight bitch. "Nigga, you not gonna help her?"

"This ain't none of my business. This between her and her man."

"You a straight bitch!" I yelled while he ran in the bedroom putting on his clothes so he could bolt before Amir could whip his ass. I kept screaming for Amir to get off Rhonda, but he was in a zone. He had Rhonda in a headlock, giving one punch after another.

I had no choice but to run up on him and jump on his back. "Leave her the fuck alone, you gon kill her." But Amir was paying me no mind. He was full of rage, and I was no match for his strength.

"Bitch, get the fuck off me." One minute I had my arm around his neck, holding on to his back, the next thing I was flying across the room, knocking over the dining room chair. The fall was so hard that as I was getting up, I stumbled back down. Rhonda's cry for help were getting weaker and weaker as Amir's beating was getting tougher and tougher. I ran into my bedroom desperate to help Rhonda. I knew with the ass whipping she was enduring she was about to be on death's door.

"Nigga, don't make me use this," I said, cocking my 9mm. "Fuckin' let her go or I guarantee I will blow you away." Amir had the nerves to try and call my bluff by punching Rhonda again. I pulled that trigger so fast and put a bullet in a glass vase that was no more than three feet away from him. "Next bullet is hitting you right between the eyes."

Amir released Rhonda so quickly she almost bumped her head on the coffee table. "If I ever catch you over here or any place in the vicinity I'm shooting first and asking questions later. Now get the fuck out!"

I kept my gun aimed ready for fire as I showed Amir the door. I made sure all the locks were in place, then ran over to Rhonda to make sure she was OK. "Thank you, Precious," Rhonda managed to say with a busted lip and two black eyes.

"Girl, that nigga did a number on you. Do you wanna call the police on him?"

"Nah, I don't feel like explaining what happened. Plus, I would hate for Amir punk ass to tell them about the gun you pulled out on him. Especially since I doubt it's registered."

"Good point. But speaking of punks, can you believe that nigga Robert? He ran outta here, not even giving a fuck that Amir was going upside your head. That's a simple ass-nigga right there."

"You got that right. But damn, Precious, how you learn to handle a gun like that?"

"I tried to tell you, Rhonda, I'm a street bitch. Where I'm from, we keep it poppin'. If this shit would've went down in my hood, instead of us sitting here putting this ice on your face, we would be trying to decide where we were going to dump the body."

"Damn, I guess I'm pretty lucky to have you as a friend. I've never met a girl that looks this great in a dress and can handle a gun like a professional hit woman."

"What can I say? I'm pretty skilled."

I sat up with Rhonda until she fell asleep on the couch. Amir had fucked her face up, but I wasn't surprised. I didn't take him for the Ike Turner type, but you never know how a man is going to react when he catch his bitch out there fucking around.

Amir's pride was hurt, but that didn't give him the right to beat Rhonda down like a dog. I would have let him slide with one bitch slap to get his woman in line, but he took it over the top. I was just relieved that I didn't have to commit my third murder, which could've easily turned into four. If I killed Amir, then more than likely I would've had to kill Rhonda. I couldn't take the chance of her slipping and confiding to someone what I did, and then I go to jail because I tried to protect her ass.

Thank goodness I didn't have to think about that because I liked Rhonda, she was cool with me.

It took damn near six weeks for Rhonda's face to get back to normal. Amir crazy ass had the audacity to call Rhonda apologizing and begging for them to try again. And Rhonda had the nerves to actually consider it, until I told her I would kick her ass if I ever saw his face up in this place. I could never understand, how women could stay with a man, knowing that at any moment you got out of line he would kick yo' ass. I guess that's what they call blinded by love, I called it stupidity.

"So, Rhonda, are you coming with me to Supreme's show tonight?"

"No, I have the worse cramps ever. You have to count me out."

"I guess I'm rolling solo."

"That's probably for the best. Maybe you'll finally get some."

"Okay. Can you believe I've been seeing this dude for two months and we still haven't fucked? But you know what's really bothering me, Rhonda?"

"What?"

"I know he's fucking somebody."

"Why you say that?"

"Sweetheart, ain't no nigga beating his beef for no two months. Nigga's need pussy like humans need food and water. I haven't figured out whether I should be flattered or offended that he's not fucking me."

Of course, after running my mouth off to Rhonda, I was late. I rushed to Madison Square Garden, hoping to catch Supreme's performance since he was closing the show, but, of course, by the time I arrived, it was over. I knew his manager was giving him an after-party at a suite in the W Hotel so I headed over there.

When I got to the penthouse floor, there were a crowd of people in the hallway mingling and drinking champagne creating their own party. The room door was open and when I entered I understood why so many people were in the hallway, it was like the disco inferno up in the bitch. It was wall-to-wall motherfuckers. I didn't see Supreme, so I weaved through the crowd hoping to spot him. I ended up in the back where there was a private sitting area. To my disgust, Supreme was sitting on the couch, talking up a storm with some bad J.Lo knockoff.

"Oh, so I guess you found someone to keep you company, huh, Supreme?"

"Precious, I'm glad you made it. I waited for you backstage, but you never came."

"So what, you scooped up the first piece of ass you could to replace me?"

"Excuse me?"

"Bitch, you heard what the fuck I said. Why don't you sit there like the good mutt you are and mind yo' business. This here is between me and Supreme."

"Listen, I don't know who you think you are, but-" before she could continue, Supreme tried to defuse the situation.

"I apologize. Precious is a very close friend of mine, and she is misreading what's going on between us, which, for the record, is nothing," he added, turning to look at me to make sure I understood.

"Fuck you, Supreme. I knew you were full of shit. Is that why you don't fuck me, 'cause you like putting your dick in bitches like her? You stay here and entertain your little friend. I'm out."

I bolted through the crowd, furious with myself. I knew I shouldn't have let myself get open off Supreme. That nigga had me playing myself in front of other bitches like I was a two-cent chick. Finally, getting through the jungle of people, I caught my breath when I reached the hallway. Numerous guys were grabbing at me as I made my way through the party, but when I laid eyes on a Mekhi Pfifer look-alike leaning against the wall, I responded to the lust in his eyes. Without as much as a hello, we locked lips and our tongues explored each other.

For that moment I wanted to forget that Supreme made me feel like a sucker and this was my way of saying fuck you.

"What the fuck are you doing?" Supreme barked as he yanked my arms from the stranger's embrace and pushed me against the wall.

"Supreme, yo' this your girl?" The Mekhi Pfifer look-alike questioned sounding like a fan.

"No, I'm just his close friend?"

"Yeah, this my girl."

"That's not what you called me when you were getting all cozy wit' miss Jenny from the block."

"Yo, shut the fuck up."

"Man, I'm sorry. I didn't know that was your girl." Somebody must've told Supreme's bodyguards there was some sort of altercation going on, because all of a sudden two big dudes came out ready to take down the Mehki Pfifer look-alike.

"Everything's cool." The boy was relieved that Supreme didn't sic his hired goons on him. "But, you can go now,"

Supreme said, brushing the guy off. Supreme grabbed my arm until we got to a door at the end of the hall. He took out a key, opened the door and pulled me into another suite. "What the fuck is wrong with you, Precious?" he said after he slammed the door.

"What the fuck is wrong wit' me? What about you. Carrying on wit' that bitch."

"We were talking, that's it. If you had got to the show on time and met me backstage like you were supposed to, then I wouldn't have to talk to nobody else."

"Oh, so now it's my fault you kicking it wit' the next bitch. I guess it's my fault, too that you don't want to have sex wit' me."

"Is that with this is about? You want me to fuck you, is that what you want, Precious? Hum, answer me." Supreme was now grabbing at me roughly, pulling on my dress. He put his hands around my waist and forcefully pushed my hips against him. "Oh, now you don't have nothing to say. Either you want me to fuck you or you don't, Precious. Which one is it?"

I remained silent because the nigga was turning me on. He then put his hands up my dress and ripped off my thong.

"How do you want me to fuck you, Precious, from the front or the back?" The next thing I knew, Supreme had me bent over a chair pounding my pussy out. My ass jiggled against his dick with each thrust.

"Oh, Supreme, baby you feel so good," I moaned.

"You was going to give all this ass to some nigga you didn't even know."

"No, baby, I was just tryna make you jealous."

"Don't lie to me."

"I swear, I only want you."

"You better 'cause this pussy is mine now. If you ever try some trifling shit like that again, I will fuck you up. You understand me?"

"Yes."

"You sure?"

"Yes, it won't neva happen again." That night I got the best dick down of my life. Now I understood why Supreme wanted to wait, because he knew once he put it on me, I would be officially sprung.

Face Off

Some good dick can do wonders for a bitch. Now that Supreme was slaying me on a regular basis, I didn't have a care in the world. I was acting all giddy for the nigga and it was bugging me out.

Rhonda instantly knew when I got some because she said my face kept a glow. Butterflies in your stomach, every time the phone ring hoping it's him, restless nights when you go to sleep without him by your side, scared that a bitch with a prettier face, bigger tits and ass will catch his eye and steal him away were the telltale signs that I heard so many girls speak of but never thought it would happen to me. I guess I was in love or deeply infatuated, one of the other. Whatever it was, I let myself enjoy the feeling and temporarily buried my insecurities of being hurt.

"Six dollars, please," the lady in the toll both screamed, interrupting my thoughts of love.

I searched for the twenty dollars I put to the side and the lady belted, "Hurry up."

"Hold on a minute," I looked out my rear view mirror and no other cars were behind me, so I didn't know why she was rushing me.

"Here you go," I said, handing her the twenty that fell on the floor by side of the door. The rude bitch snatched the money from me like she owned the George Washington Bridge. After she damn near tossed my change at me, I said, "Bitch, don't get mad at me 'cause you working at a toll booth. If you don't like it, get another job."

"Watch yo' mouth, you stank hoe."

I couldn't let that Jheri-curl having bitch get away with that. I stuck my head out the window and spit dead in her face. She reached her hand out and tried to grab my neck. I pressed down so hard on the gas and sped off before she tried to flag down the cop. But that's what she got for popping all that shit.

After crossing the bridge, I turned onto the Henry Hudson Parkway downtown on my way to meet Supreme at the studio. I looked at the clock and saw that I was running mad early, so I decided to stop by my old apartment on 142nd and Riverside. The tollbooth lady still had me riled up and I needed to cool down, plus, I hadn't been there in months and wanted to check on the spot. I thought about sub-leasing it, since Inga wasn't staying there,, but I didn't need the money, and I liked knowing that I always had a place to crash, if need be.

When I finally found a parking spot, I walked up to the building and noticed that it had been painted recently. The super was maintaining the building well, and I knew that must of meant he would be raising the rent again soon. I took the elevator to the seventh floor, and although this place didn't have all the amenities of the spot I lived in Jersey, I somewhat missed living here. It was my very first apartment, so it held a lot of sentimental value.

I heard loud music as soon as I stepped off the elevator. When I lived here, I remembered it being so quiet, so I was surprised. Everyone on my floor was either old or married with young children. When I got closer to my door, I realized the music was coming from my apartment. I put the key in and when I tried to open it, the chain blocked any further entrance. I heard a female voice scream over the music, "Is that you, Inga?"

"Hun, humm," I grumbled loudly. *I know Inga's trifling ass is not staying here. That bitch told me she was keeping her ass in Brooklyn at her mom's crib. But who the fuck is in there, Inga ain't got no sister,* I thought to myself.

I was heated at the idea of somebody chilling in my crib. I reached in my purse and pulled out the knife I always kept on me. I stepped away from the door so whoever opened it couldn't see me if they looked through the peep hole. The moment I heard the girl take off the chain, I grabbed the knob and pushed the door open. The door knocked the girl in the head, and she let out a yelp and covered her face. Without missing a beat, I slammed the door shut and jumped on top of the girl, pinned her arms down with my knees and put the knife to her throat. When I saw who it was, my first instinct was to slit her throat, but I needed to get some answers first.

"Porscha, what the fuck are you doing in my apartment?" She was still in pain from the door smashing her face that there was a long, pregnant pause before she focused on answering my question.

"I knew I should've had those locks changed," were the first words out the bitch's mouth.

"Bitch, you got bigger problems than that right now. How long has Inga been letting you stay in my crib?" Porscha dumb-ass rolled her eyes as if she had no intentions on answering my question. I put the tip of my knife to her throat and nipped it just deep enough to draw blood. She let out an involuntary scream, and I covered her mouth with my hand. "Listen to me, you two-dollar whore. I have no problem ending your life right now. So you can either answer my fucking questions or say your last prayer."

"What do you want to know," Porscha managed to say under sniffles.

"Start by telling me how long Inga been letting you stay here."

"About three months ago she gave me the key. She said you gave her the apartment."

"Now why the fuck would yo' dumbass want to lie up in my spot when you know I can't stand your motherfucking ass."

"At first, Nico told me to stop through because he wanted to see if you stashed his million dollars here. Inga and I came to look, but we didn't find it. Then she called asking you about the money, and you told her you didn't know what she was talking about. I told Nico, but he said you were lying. He told me to ask Inga if I could chill here for awhile, just in case you came through."

"Well, bitch, I'm here now, what you supposed to do?"

"For the first few weeks Nico had a couple of his boys stationed out front, watching everyday and night for you to show up, ready to do whatever to get his money back. After awhile we decided you was ghost and wasn't coming back, so Nico told his boys to forget about it. But I like having my own place, so I decided to stay."

"When you say Nico told his boys to do whatever in order to get his money, you mean kill me?"

"No, that was one thing he instructed them not to do. He said killing you was the one pleasure he would save for himself."

"Nico locked up for damn near the rest of his life. How the fuck is he ever gonna get that pleasure?"

"How the fuck I know? That nigga so crazy he's determined that somehow he will get out of jail."

"Why does Nico believe I have his money?"

"One of Nico's street informants told him that word had it that Tommy tried to cross him and went to his crib to steal the million. It wasn't there but Tommy got some information from Boogie's nephews that they were supposed to meet up wit' this chick, which was you, to make the paper clean. Something went wrong because Boogie, Tommy and the nephews all ended up dead but the money was neva found. So Nico said you still had it. When he got locked up, the streets turned on him and stole all his money. That million was the only paper he had left, and he wanted it back."

"Answer me this, Porscha. Did Nico have my mother killed?"

I always thought Tommy and Boogie's nephews killed my mother, but I could never explain how they got in her apartment. The door wasn't broken, so whoever did it, my mother let them in. That didn't make sense to me because of the lifestyle my mother lived. She wouldn't open the door for nobody unless she knew you and was expecting you. So if Tommy and his boys showed up unexpectedly, they would've had to kick in the door to get to her.

"I don't know if you ready for this, Precious."

"Porscha, don't talk to me in riddles. If I'm asking the questions, then I want the answers."

"You can't say I didn't try to warn you. Nico's street informant was Inga. Her and Tommy was cool, and he told her that the nephews told him that Boogie told them that you had the million dollars.

"Inga tried to find out where you were so she could tell Tommy, but you wouldn't give her no information. So then Inga told Tommy that you might've stashed the money at your mom's crib. Inga also knew how your mom's didn't answer the door for nobody, and Tommy didn't want to cause no loud raucous kicking in the door 'cause he figured somebody might call the police. He told Inga that if she would knock on the door, acting like she was looking for you, then he would hit her off with seventy-five thousand."

"Did Inga know that Tommy and them were going to kill my mom's?"

"She figured they would, but she said yo' mom's was a crackhead anyway, and them killing her would put her out of her misery." I couldn't believe what Porscha was telling me, although it all made sense. I knew Inga felt betrayed about that sorry-ass nigga Ritchie, but to let Tommy and them kill my mother was the lowest you could go. Inga knew that as much hell as my mother put me through, she was all I had my entire life. To take her away from me was stealing my last breath.

"How could Inga do that to my mother?" I asked myself out loud.

"Precious, you know Inga blames you for her fucked-up life. She believes you fucked up her relationship with Ritchie and is responsible for Nico killing him, leaving her without a father for her son. She's barely making ends meet and her mother the one that have to watch the baby while she at work."

"What happened to the fifty thousand I gave her?"

"Didn't she tell you she bought a car, clothes, jewelry and shit."

"Why don't she sell her fucking car, so she can have some damn money for the baby?"

"She totaled it in a car accident and her dumb ass let the car insurance lapse."

"Where is Inga at right now?"

"She was supposed to be on her way over here, but I'm not sure."

"Call her now and find out exactly where she at. Also find out if the baby wit' her."

"I need my cell phone."

"Where is it?"

"Right over there on that nightstand."

"Porscha, I'ma let you up so you can get your phone, but I'm keeping this knife right under your throat. If I even think you gonna try some slick shit, I'm slitting side to side. Do you understand?"

She nodded her head. I hoped the fear was instilled in her to the point that she would do as I said. It's not like I cared whether the bitch lived or died, but I did need her to get to Inga. Porscha dialed Inga's number and did exactly as I asked. When she hung up she informed me that Inga was still in Brooklyn at her mom's crib. "Let's go."

"Where we going?"

"To Brooklyn to pay a visit to my dear old friend Inga."

"Precious, I don't want no part of that. You crazy and there ain't no telling what you gonna do."

"You right. So you want to take me to Inga or should I

kill you right now?"

Porscha grabbed her shoes and phone, and we went to the car. We stopped at my trunk so I could get my 9mm, then I made Porscha get on the driver's side. I kept my gun pointed at her the whole time. On our drive to Brooklyn, I kept imagining how my mother must've felt when she realized Inga had set her up. Your daughter's so-called best friend being an accessory in your death.

When Porscha pulled up to the projects Inga lived in, I scanned the area looking for the best spot to have our show-down. "Drive around to that back parking lot." That parking lot was always isolated, because the hustler's needed to be where the action was, and the dope fiends needed to be near the dealers, so nobody ever came back there.

"Now what?" an exasperated Porscha questioned.

"Call Inga. Tell her that I unexpectedly showed up at the crib with the money, we got into it, and you stabbed me to death. Say you left my body at the apartment and took my car and the money. Then tell her you need her help and to come outside because you're in the back parking lot."

"What's going to happen after that?"

"If you promise not to mention a word to anyone about everything you told me and what I'm about to do to Inga, then I'll let you walk away from this whole situation alive. But you have to promise me that first."

"I promise, Precious. I won't say a word. I'll pretend like today neva even happened."

"You can't even tell Nico."

"I won't. I don't even fuck wit' Nico like that. He so obsessed wit' you that he only uses me to keep tabs on what I hear on the streets. I don't even like taking his collect calls no more because the first question he ask me is if I heard what nigga you supposed to be fucking wit.

"That shit was getting on my nerves. I was the one going to court to support him and brought him clothes so he wouldn't sit through trial in that nasty ass orange jumpsuit, spending my money on car rentals so I could go visit his ass in jail. I was writing him letters and having to suck dick to get the money to pay for the high-ass phone bills, I had for accepting his collect calls. I did all that shit for that nigga and he want to sit on the phone and vent about the chick that caused him to get locked up in the first place. So, no, you definitely don't have to worry about me telling Nico. I don't need to give him another reason to go on and on about you."

"Good. Now call Inga."

Porscha kicked the speech that we rehearsed and Inga fell for it hook, line and sinker. I heard her devious ass screaming with glee when Porscha told her she had the money. Not at one point did she show any remorse or sympathy for me when Porsha said I was dead. She actually laughed and exclaimed, "Good. That bitch had it coming."

"Her mom was walking in when we were about to get off the phone. She said she had to throw on some clothes and she would be out in five minutes." Porscha explained after hanging up with Inga.

"OK, let's go."

"Where we going now?"

"I don't want her to see me in the car. Let's go stand over there underneath the stairwell opening."

"I thought you said after I called Inga, I was done and could leave."

"When we see her coming, all I want you to do is call

her name and show your face, then you can bounce. Is that too much to ask?"

"Nah, I can handle that." We got out the car, and I kept the gun on Porscha as we walked towards our destination. "You can put the gun away now, Precious. I ain't gonna try to run off. I'll stay wit' you until Inga come outside. You gon kill her, not me."

"True, but you can never be too careful."

Porscha and I turned our heads simultaneously in the same direction at the sound of someone's footsteps. We both assumed it was Inga, and I nodded my head giving Porscha the sign to call out her name.

"Inga, is that you?"

"Yeah, where you at?"

"Right over here by the stairs," Porscha replied. I stepped out of sight, waiting for Inga to come closer.

"Girl, I'm so excited I can't believe you got all that paper. I can finally quit that damn job at the nursing home," Inga said as the sound of her voice became louder as she got closer to Porscha.

I stepped from behind the brick wall that was shielding me, and would've done anything to have forever captured the look on Inga's face when she saw me. "Aren't you happy to see your best friend, Inga?"

"Porscha, you set me up!"

"I ain't have no choice. She was gonna kill me if I didn't get you out here."

"Both of you stand over here," I said, pointing my gun in the direction I wanted them to move.

"Precious, I don't know what Porscha told you but its all lies."

"Save it, Inga. I heard wit' my own ears how excited you were at the news that I was dead. But I could even let that go. What I can't let go is that you set my mother up to die at the hands of Tommy and his boys."

Inga turned and glared at Porscha with hate.

"Don't look at me," Porscha said, crossing her arms and rolling her head.

"Precious, I didn't know Tommy was gonna kill your moms. I thought he was going in there to just try and find the money."

"You lying bitch. Porscha, repeat what you said Inga told you about my mother."

"She said yo' mom's was a crack head anyway and them killing her would put her out of her misery. That's what the fuck you said, Inga."

"You know what's so foul about that, Inga. When my mother opened that door you could look at her and tell she wasn't using drugs no more. I saw her earlier that day and she was more beautiful than ever.

"But you didn't care. All you wanted was yo' funky seventy-five thousand dollars. But I'll tell you what I'll do for you. I'll give that money to your mother to take care of your son. Think of it as her cashing in your life insurance policy."

"Precious, I'm so sorry. Please don't kill me. I was just hurt over the whole Ritchie situation. I fucked up, but we can get pass all this." The tears were swelling in Inga's eyes as she begged for her life.

"I think it's time for me to go head and leave now and let ya handle your business. But like we discussed, Precious, didn't none of this happen. All this stay between me and you."

"Sorry, Porscha. I had a change of heart. All of this stays with me, not you." I aimed the gun right and center where her mouth dropped when she heard the news. It all happened so fast, she couldn't even close it before I pulled the trigger. Her whole head damn near came off. "You know I neva liked that bitch."

By this time Inga was on her hands and knees as if I would show any mercy for her.

"Precious, please, it's not too late. We can start all over; get the fuck out of Brooklyn, you, me and little Ritchie."

"Tell me you didn't name your son after a nigga who didn't give a fuck about you or his seed. Bitch, I'ma kill you just for that."

With that, I put two bullets in Inga. One for the death of my mother, the other for being a stupid cunt for naming her son after his trifling father. I left the two dead snakes lying beside one another. Neither one of them bitches would be having an open casket at their funeral.

He'll Be Back

Supreme had been furious with me since the day I killed Porscha and Inga. I was supposed to have met him at the studio, and he blew my phone up and left a ton of messages when I never came. Then he kept calling Rhonda because he started getting scared, thinking something terrible had happened to me.

When I finally called him, my brain was so fried I couldn't come up with a reasonable explanation for disappearing for all those hours. He kept saying be honest and just tell him the truth. But I couldn't seem to come up with a way to say I was out committing two murders. That's when he told me he didn't want to speak to me until I told him exactly where I had been. I was actually relieved. I had killed before, but I couldn't get murdering Inga out of my head.

A week after Inga' funeral, I kept my word and made sure her mother got hundred thousand dollars for the care of little Ritchie. I gave an extra twenty-five thousand for my guilt because, however justified I felt, I was responsible for him growing up not ever knowing his mother or father. The least I could do was give some money to hopefully help the boy have a chance at a future. Inga's mom was always a hard worker and good woman. She wouldn't go blow all the cash on material shit. She would make sure the baby was provided for.

With everything that happened and Supreme not speaking to me, I was becoming restless. My days were getting longer and my nights shorter. I wasn't doing nothing with myself. "Girl, get out the bed," Rhonda said as she disturbed what had now become the norm for me, sleeping my time away.

"What is it, Rhonda?"

"Wake up and do something. I'm starting to think you're a vampire. You sleep all day and watch television all night. Let's go out and have some drinks or something."

"I'm not up to it."

"You better start. Do you think Supreme laying around in his bed mourning over you?"

"I'm not mourning over Supreme. I'm just in a funk. I have a lot of shit on my mind."

"Well snap out of it. Get dressed. Let's go to the city." Rhonda was right. I'd been dragging my body around here in a daze. Being on the outs with Supreme was bothering me more than I wanted to admit.

The few times I tried to call him, he said unless I was going to come clean with him, then he had nothing to say to me. He was so not checking for me the last couple of times I called, he let it go to voicemail. I didn't understand why he was tripping so hard. I swore to him I wasn't with another dude or anything, but that day I had an unexpected emergency that needed to be handled. His problem was that I didn't have family and I didn't have a job so what type of emergency could keep me away from him where I couldn't at least call? As bad as I wanted to believe that Supreme would get over this, he was so fucking stubborn; the reality that he might not be back was setting in.

That night Rhonda took me to some lounge called Duvet. There were beds scattered throughout the place with a bar designed to look like a block of ice. It was the typical crowd, mixed with models, actors, industry heads and beautiful people. The hostess sat us at a bed in the corner next to Cam'ron and his crew. Rhonda was mingling at their bed because she was real cool with his manager.

I sat there sipping on my drink, wishing I could crawl back in my own real bed. I was in no mood to be out and about, but to my devastation, Supreme was. I couldn't help but notice when he walked in the spot with a girl on his arm. She looked like some chick I'd seen in a music video or something. They sat on a bed on the other side of the room but still within my viewing area. His two bodyguards parked themselves on the bed beside them.

Seeing Supreme with that girl felt like someone stabbed me in the heart, twisted it and then left the shit on automatic rotate. The pain was so continuous it seemed it would never stop. "Precious, are you OK? You have this expression on your face like you're stuck in a nightmare."

"That sounds about right. I guess you didn't see Supreme walk in."

"No, where is he?"

"Right over there." I pointed at the bed across from us. He was in such deep conversation with his date that he hadn't even looked in my direction yet.

"I told you not to be sitting around mourning over his ass. Maybe you'll finally snap out of that coma you've been in for the last few weeks."

I looked up at Rhonda and then looked back at myself.

I had to make sure I was hearing what I thought I heard. Rhonda was actually giving me a pep talk. When that sunk in, the fire that used to burn inside of me suddenly reignited. My eyes zoomed in on the dude poppin' bottles who had been sizing me up since I sat down.

"Do you know who that is?" I asked pointing towards the dude on the low.

"Hell yeah, that's pretty boy Mike. He owns Pristine Records."

There was no need for Rhonda to explain why they called him "Pretty Boy"; the nigga was fine. But what set him off was that even though he was pretty, you could also tell that he was a straight-up thug. Trying to be discreet didn't work because after Rhonda said her piece, pretty boy Mike approached our bed.

"You mind if I sit on your bed?"

"Nah, have a seat."

"I know you seen me watching you since you stepped in the place. I didn't think you were interested until I noticed you point me out to your friend."

"Damn, you saw that? I was tryna be tactful. I guess it didn't work. But how you know I wasn't clowning you to my friend?"

"I didn't, but the fact you acknowledged my presence gave me the confidence to introduce myself to you. I'm Mike and your name is," he said, extending his hand out to me.

"Nice to meet you, Mike. My name is Precious."

"It's a pleasure to meet you. Do you live here in the city?"

"No, I rep Brooklyn, but I live in Jersey now."

"Brooklyn girl. What part of Brooklyn is you from?"

"I used to live over there in Riverdale Towers."

"Damn, that's hard knock. You look more Brooklyn Heights than Riverdale Towers."

"Don't let the face, clothes and jewelry fool you. I'm BK to the fullest."

"You know what, Precious? I believe you."

"Why's that?"

"You so damn gorgeous, I didn't even pay attention to the darkness in your eyes. That's deadly. A man has to be on top of his game to deal with you. You know I live in Jersey, but I, too, come from the school of hard knocks. I've been around these Hollywood acting cats for so long that I'm slipping. I couldn't even recognize one of my own."

"Yeah, you are slipping because when my girlfriend told me they called you pretty boy Mike, I said to myself, Yeah he might be pretty, but he's a straight up thug. These simple-ass niggas around here don't see that in you but I do."

Mike put his hand on my cheek and gently rubbed the side of my face.

"You my type of girl, Precious, beautiful on the outside but tough as nails on the inside."

"Precious, I need to speak to you." It took me a minute to focus 'cause pretty boy Mike's game was kinda tight. Eventually, I came too and Supreme was standing in front of me.

"What up, Supreme?" Mike said, extending his hand but quickly putting it back down when Supreme made it clear he was showing no love.

"What do you want?" I snapped.

"To speak to you."

"Whateva you have to say, you can say it right here."

"You wanna act cute, that's cool. What the fuck are you

doing over here with this nigga."

"Yo, man, there is no need for you to get all excited. Chill out."

"Pretty boy Mike, this ain't none of your business, I'm having a conversation with my girl."

"Your girl? That's hard to tell when you came in here wit' some chick."

"So is that why you letting this nigga touch all on your face 'cause you seen me with a female? That's not acceptable. Get yo' shit, and let's go."

"I'm not going anywhere with you, Supreme. You not answering my calls, you been lounging on the bed ever since you swaggered in here with some other bitch and now you tryna dictate what the fuck I'm supposed to do. Kiss my ass. I'm staying right where the fuck I'm at."

Supreme reached down and grabbed my arm, trying to pull me off the bed. That's when Mike stepped in and pushed Supreme out the way, and all hell broke lose. Supreme's bodyguards swarmed in and attacked Mike. Then the three guys that came with Mike ran over and started busting bottles over the bodyguards heads. With all the commotion going on, Supreme grabbed my arm and practically dragged me out the club. We hopped in the Suburban that was waiting out front with him cussing at me the whole time.

"What happened to your little arm piece that you came in here with?"

"When I spotted you getting all up close and personal with that nigga Mike, I knew it was about to be some trouble so I gave her some money to take a cab home."

"So what is she supposed to be your new girlfriend?"

"No, just someone who was keeping me company while

my girlfriend was supposed to be getting her mind right. But instead you was up in Duvet, getting cozy with some industry cat. I was about to bust yo' ass in there."

"I don't know why. You the one that's been giving me straight shade for the last few weeks. Do you know how sick at the stomach I was when I saw you come in the club with that girl? I thought I lost you for good."

"Honestly, Precious, when you wouldn't tell me what was going on with you I was leaning towards cutting you off. But when I saw you with that nigga I lost it. The thought of some other man in my pussy was about to make me go ballistic. We gotta find a way to work this out 'cause I can't give you up."

When we got back to my place, the first thing I did after locking the door was unzipped Supreme's jeans and put his dick in my mouth. I wanted to taste him so bad, and I also wanted him to remember what my lips felt like wrapped around his manhood. I was in love with Supreme, and I didn't ever want to worry again if he would leave me and never come back.

Death Do Us Part

Once again I was feeling alive after the thug lovin' Supreme put on me. The love I felt for Supreme was becoming so strong, that I considered him to be the man I wanted to spend the rest of my life with. Because of that, I debated whether or not I should come clean with him about my past.

Of course, not tell him everything, but enough for him to get a general idea about who I am. Or maybe who I was. Falling in love was beginning to soften my heart and make me want to change my ways. All my life, the only person I could depend on was me. Nobody had my back or gave a fuck about me. Everybody was out for self, including me. It was different now; everything had changed. I knew that Supreme was in love with me like I was in love with him. For the first time somebody valued my life and genuinely cared what happened to me.

I woke up famished and went to the kitchen. "Rhonda, what you doing here, why aren't you at work?"

"By the time I got home after escaping from all the drama you caused, I was too tired to go to work."

"Escape, how long did that shit last after we left?"

"They had to shut the club down. The fight between Mike and his people and Supreme's bodyguards spilled over to some other niggas. Pretty soon the whole club was basically fighting. The police had to come in and break that shit up. Thank goodness I had your car keys because when I looked around your ass was nowhere to be found."

"As soon as the fight broke out, Supreme got me outta there."

"Yeah, when I got home early this morning I saw his driver sitting in the car, waiting for him. I guess that means ya kissed and made up."

"Something like that." My face was beaming as I smiled from ear to ear. "So what happened to that dude Mike? Was he a'ight?"

"Yeah, he escaped out of there around the same time as me. His face was still intact. Supreme's bodyguards got pretty fucked up 'cause them dudes were busting bottles. That was some crazy shit."

"What exactly do you know about Mike?"

"Damn, Precious I thought you just said that you and Supreme were back together. You want to fuck it up and start seeing Mike too."

"No, it's nothing like that. I'm in love wit' Supreme I'm not doing nothing to fuck that up."

"Then why the interest in Mike?"

"Something about the conversation we had last night bothered me. It wasn't anything specific. A few things he said seemed odd."

"What things?"

"I can't really pinpoint it. The conversation in general. So what do you know about him?"

"Not much. He came on the scene a couple of years ago, making big moves. The first couple of artist he put out just went straight to the top of the chart, selling millions of albums. He quickly solidified himself as bigwig in the music business. People respect him. He don't cause no trouble."

"Interesting, sounds like an overnight success story."

"You can say that, and oh, yeah, he's also from Brooklyn," Rhonda added before going to her bedroom. Maybe that's what it was; certain Brooklyn niggas got this way about them. Dudes from other boroughs don't exude it. I couldn't put my finger on it, but something about pretty boy Mike I couldn't shake.

Later on that day, I got dressed because I was going to the city to meet Supreme. He was having a session at Sony Music Studio and I was determined to be on time. We were finally back on track and I wasn't going to do anything to jeopardize that. I was also looking forward to going because I had never been inside a studio before.

When I turned on 54th street, there was a Bentley in front and a couple of Benz's, Beamers and Range Rovers lined on the side of the street. It looked more like a car show than a place of business. I parked my car in the lot because I wasn't taking chances getting my shit towed.

"Hi, I'm here for Supreme's session."

"Your name?"

"Precious."

"Hold on one moment." The guy got on the phone and I assumed he was calling the studio to make sure it was OK for me to go in the session. "Sign in and go right through those doors, he's in studio A."

I followed the guy's directions and came to the door that had the letter A. When I opened the heavy wood door, I entered into a lounge. There were a few black leather couches and a television with a play station hooked up. A whole bunch of junk food was sitting on a table off to the side and mini-refrigerator was next to it.

I stayed on course and followed the loud music, which led me to the actual studio. The lights were dim, but I could see somebody in the vocal booth messing with his head phones. The guy didn't look like Supreme, though. Then a couple of guys that were hauled up in the corner smoking weed noticed me.

"Who you looking for, Mami?"

"Supreme. Is this his session?"

"Nah, this the wrong studio."

"Is this studio A?"

"Yeah, but I believe Supreme in Studio B. It's right across the hall."

"Thanks. Sorry about that."

"No problem. You more than welcome to stay," the weed smoker said in attempt to flirt with me.

"Maybe another time." As I turned to walk away, pretty boy Mike was standing in my way.

"Precious Cummings, I was hoping to run into you again. I wasn't counting on seeing you so soon though." I didn't recall telling Mike my last name, 'cause honestly I'm not really deep on conversation to do all that.

"Well, here I am. I'm glad I did run into. I wanted to apologize for what happened last night."

"Things happen. It wasn't your fault."

"Appreciate that. Thanks for being so cool. Well I better be going."

"You here to see Supreme?"

"Yes, the guy upfront accidentally sent me to the wrong studio."

"I'll walk you out."

"That's OK. I can find my way."

"But I wanted to talk to you about a mutual friend of ours."

"You must be mistaken 'cause I don't know any of your friends."

"Oh, I could've sworn you knew Nico Carter." I wanted to come up with some sort of quick denial but I couldn't. I was stunned that of all the people in the state of New York, our mutual friend had to be my worse enemy.

"As a matter of fact, I do know Nico, but from a long time ago."

"Come have a seat, Precious. We should talk."

"I don't have time. Supreme is waiting for me."

"Make time." Mike was making it clear that this wasn't a request, but more so a demand. I followed him into the lounge and sat on one of the black leather couches I had observed on my way in.

"What do you want?" I said defensively.

"Remember last night when we were talking and you told me that you rep for BK."

I nodded my head, letting him know I remembered saying it, but now wishing I hadn't.

"Then I told you I was slipping because I didn't even recognize my own. I meant that in terms of identifying the wifey of a kingpin."

"Don't worry 'bout it, 'cause I ain't nobody's wifey, especially not a kingpin's."

"Let me finish, Precious," he said sternly. "See before I got in this music game, I was a kingpin. Unlike so many fallen soldiers, I was able to get out and take my money and make it legitimate. But the streets still run through my blood.

So, I should always be able to spot another soldier, which includes a wifey. A wifey is an intricate element to a kingpin. A wifey has the eyes of death because they're always a step away from it. The only time I've ever seen that look in a woman's eyes was right before I killed my own wifey-that is until I looked in yours.

"That was so many years ago, and I'd forgotten because there aren't that many true kingpins, so there aren't many women who are truly built to be the wifey of a kingpin."

"So why did you kill your wifey?" I asked with curiosity.

"She didn't remain loyal. She caught me fucking around so to retaliate she fucked around on me. Of course, she had to die. It destroyed me to end her life, but her body was no longer sacred. Part of me died when I killed her; she was my everything. I molded her to be tough as nails on the inside, just like you, Precious. But, see, her mistake was she tried to teach the teacher a lesson."

"This makes for an interesting conversation, but what is your point in telling me all this bullshit?"

"Nico Carter is a true kingpin and you are his wifey. No matter who is supposed to be your man, you still belong to Nico until death do you part. The only reason why you're still alive, Precious, is because only Nico can end your life, and he will when he gets out. That is my message to you."

"Lucky for me, Nico will be in jail for the rest of his life. Let me ask you a question, Mike? Did you know all this before you was pushing up on me at da club?"

"I truly admire the fire in you, Precious?"

"Answer the damn question."

"As you know, Nico garners a lot of respect on the

streets, and we were all aware of his incarceration. The top heads soon learned you were the reason for his demise, but at his request everyone agreed to let him handle you personally. I knew your name, but I'd never seen you before. When you walked into the club I was mesmerized by you.

"My wifey was beautiful but nowhere near your caliber. When I came over and introduced myself, I thought you were in the entertainment industry. But then when you said you were from Brooklyn and you told me your name, something clicked. The first thing I did this morning was investigate. It didn't take long to put all the pieces together. You're still a baby and yet you're already a legend in Brooklyn."

"So what I'm supposed to be? Grateful for this little speech you just gave me?"

"As I tried to explain, I'm just the messenger giving you a warning."

"You mean a death sentence."

"I know Nico taught you the code of the streets. You didn't honestly believe you could walk away from him. There's always a price to pay, and it usually means death."

"Are you finished because Supreme is waiting for me?"

"We're done here."

"Good, and by the way, next time you speak to Nico, deliver a message for me. Tell him I hope he rots in jail for the rest of his life."

My heart was beating so fast. I didn't want Mike to know it, but what he said had me petrified. I reached a point in my life where I had a reason to live, and here he was, delivering the news that death was right around the corner. My hands were shaking, and I was visibly upset. I didn't want to go in Supreme's session looking so distraught. I stopped in the bathroom and splashed water on my face. I dabbed on some fresh lip gloss, trying to erase the look of defeat away. I held out my hands and the shaking wouldn't stop. "I give up. Fuck it."

"Where have you been? They called in the studio a half hour ago saying you were here."

I was surprised to see Supreme standing in the middle of the hallway.

"Baby, the guy gave me the wrong studio. I sat in the lounge for over fifteen minutes before someone told me the correct room. By that time I had to use the bathroom so bad. I'm sorry I had you waiting."

"That's cool. I just worry about you. All these vultures around here, I would hate for one of them to take you away," he said, kissing me on the forehead. "What the fuck is that nigga doing here?" I looked up and saw Mike.

"Precious, I see that you found Supreme."

Supreme eyed me suspiciously.

"Baby, studio A, the session that Mike is in, was the wrong room I accidentally went into. Mike was nice enough to point me in the right direction. Thanks again."

"No problem. Supreme I hope there are no hard feelings about what went down last night; I heard your bodyguards were in pretty bad shape."

"Nah, they recovering nicely, but I got two more here with me now, until they recover a hundred percent. Would you like to meet them?"

"No, thanks I'll take your word. But with a girl as gorgeous as Precious on your arm, you might need two more. It would be a shame for someone to come take her away."

"Nigga, stay away from her." Supreme and Mike were

now standing toe to toe.

"Supreme, stop. Lets just go. He didn't mean nothing by it." I was holding onto Supreme's arm, praying he would back down. He had no idea he was butting heads with a killer.

"I think you should take your woman's advice."

I finally got Supreme to walk away, but not before Mike said, "Precious, I'll make sure to tell Nico you said hello."

"Who is Nico?"

"Nobody important. Just some dude that we both know from Brooklyn."

"Precious, I don't ever want you talking to Mike again. If you see him go in the opposite direction, 'cause that nigga rubs me the wrong way." Supreme didn't have to say anymore, I had already come to that very same conclusion.

Holy Matrimony

For the third night in a row I woke up in a pool of sweat, suffering from the same nightmare. I'm at a funeral and my mother, Boogie, Nico, Ritchie, Butch, Azar, Boogie's nephews, Tommy, Porscha and Inga are all there dressed in black. I'm the only one in white.

I walk over to my mother, but it's like she can't see me. No one can see me. Then they all gather around the casket that is about to be lowered into the ground. I slowly move forward to get a glimpse of the person we gathered here to mourn and to my horror it's me. I blamed Mike for my delusions, and it made me angry. In a twenty-minute conversation, he managed to turn my whole world upside down.

"Precious, telephone. It's Supreme," Rhonda yelled out, helping to shake my terror.

"Hi, baby."

"You still in the bed, sleepyhead?"

"I'm getting up now."

"What are you doing later on?"

"Hopefully I'ma see you."

"Cool 'cause I wanted to take you out to dinner tonight."

"Really, where?"

"You'll see. Wear something really nice and sexy, of course."

I was so happy Supreme planned a romantic outing for

us. I could now focus on something other than death.

After speaking to Supreme, I had the energy to get out of bed and eat some breakfast. "Good morning, Rhonda."

"Good morning, Supreme called pretty early this morning."

"He wanted to tell me that he planned a romantic dinner for us tonight."

"Nice, things have gotten really serious between you guys."

"I know, so serious that I think it's time for me to sit down and let him into my life."

"What do you mean?"

"Rhonda, there are a lot of things about me that you don't know and neither does Supreme. I don't trust people and because of that, I keep most things to myself. That way no one can hurt me. But since I've fallen in love with Supreme, I want to share my world with him."

"That's so passionate, Precious. I'm impressed."

"Rhonda, this isn't funny."

"I wasn't joking, I'm serious, Precious. I think it's totally amazing that you're going to open up to Supreme. I could always tell that you were different, but I didn't want to intrude in your life. You appear to be perfect on the outside, but you've made it clear that the inside is a lot more complex. Not to mention the way you was about to put it on Amir. I've never seen anything like that before. I'll always be grateful to you for standing up for me."

"Thanks, Rhonda. You pretty cool yourself. You did take me in as a roommate without even knowing me."

"That's called desperation, and the nine thousand dollars upfront didn't hurt."

We fell out laughing because it was the truth.

"I'm glad I was desperate, though, because you turned out to be the best roommate ever. You're unlike any friend I've ever had. Your feelings, thoughts, are all so real. In my world that quality is an endangered species. I'm keeping my fingers crossed because I truly hope that everything works out for you and Supreme and you all have a wonderful life together."

"Me too."

I spent the rest of the day preparing for my evening with Supreme. I went to Elaine's in Edgewater Commons for a complete spa treatment. I then took it over to my beautician to get my tresses in order. By the time I got home, it was time for me to get dressed. I put on a deep v-neck plunged white dress, that had stone and bead detailing, which added a little sparkle. The length fell right above my knees and dangerously hugged every curve.

"Damn. When Supreme sees you in that dress he might ask you to marry him tonight," Rhonda said when I strutted in the living room.

"Girl, you so crazy."

"Call me crazy if you like, but you look like a goddess. No one would ever guess you can handle a gun better than a dude."

"Let that be our little secret."

"Do you know where Supreme is taking you?"

"Not yet." I was giving myself the once over in the hallway mirror when the phone rang.

"Your Prince has arrived," Rhonda announced. I grabbed my purse anxious to see Supreme. "Have fun tonight."

"I will." I couldn't get downstairs fast enough. The elevator seemed to be going so slow, but I knew it was only because I was so anxious. When I got outside, my chariot awaited me in the form of a silver Maybach. The driver was holding the backseat passenger door open for me and Supreme stepped out with the most beautiful bouquet of flowers. He had on a linen white suit, which matched perfectly with my white dress. A tear rolled down my cheek, but this time it wasn't out of pain. It was pure love.

I was so busy making out with Supreme in the backseat like we were in high school, I didn't pay attention to where we were going. So when we arrived at what looked to be an airport, I was confused. "Baby, where are we?"

"Teterboro Airport."

"What are we doing here?"

"They're fueling up the private jet. We're having dinner on the beach in Barbados."

"Are you serious? I've never been on a private jet before or dinner in Barbados. I can't believe you're doing this for me."

"I wanted this night to be special."

During the flight I kept pinching myself because this couldn't be real. My life seemed to be going too perfectly- no drama with bitches, no drama with my man and nobody getting killed. It didn't seem like my life; it was like I stepped into someone else's. It was fine with me. I was ready to leave that street life behind. Who knew that a drama-free life could be so much fun?

When the jet landed a car was waiting to take us to a yacht. Then the yacht took us to a private beach where dinner was served. A path of rose pedals led to our table in the center of a glass gazebo surrounded by vandella roses and pink peony flowers. Flat dishes filled with sand displayed vanilla candles. A mini orchestra dressed in tuxedos was playing the most soothing music.

We even had a wait staff to serve us our meal and keep the champagne flowing. Coming from the bottom I never imagined what heaven was like, but this had to be it. "Supreme, I never thought I could be speechless. This is amazing."

"You're amazing. Precious, I'm in love with you. I want to spend the rest of my life with you."

"Before you say anything else, there is something I want to tell you."

"You sound so serious. What is it?"

"I don't know exactly where to start."

"The beginning would be fine."

"It's a little more complicated than that."

"Precious, just tell me, don't hold back." I took a deep breath, trying to prepare for this moment. I wasn't sure how Supreme was going to react to what I had to say, but I knew it needed to be done. It was only fitting that I purge my soul in the middle of paradise.

"As you know I'm from Brooklyn. I grew up in the projects, depending on no one but myself. Because of my mother's drug addiction, she left me no choice but to go out there and make money to support us and, in her case, support her drug habit.

So, at the age of fifteen, I started fucking around with hustlers so they could take care of me and I could bring money home to my moms. In doing that I got caught up in a lot of bullshit, and I became cold. 'Cause when you out in those streets, don't nobody give a fuck about you. I soon met a man by the name of Nico Carter."

"Nico? Is that the guy Mike mentioned when we were

in the studio?"

"Yes. I lied when I told you he was nobody. He's actually my ex-boyfriend who is currently locked up doing life in prison for a murder I set up."

"What!"

"You heard me. He cheated on me and I wanted to teach him a lesson so I started having sex with his best friend Ritchie, and I made sure he found out because I knew he would flip out and kill him."

"Wait a minute, I remember that case. That happened not too long ago. It was in the paper almost every day. Nico Carter was some big time kingpin from Brooklyn. He was convicted of killing two guys. They said it was over some drug operation gone bad, but you're saying it wasn't that at all."

"No, it wasn't. It was all my doing. I wanted to make sure he spent the rest of his life in prison."

"But he was convicted of killing two guys. He killed his best friend for fucking around with you, but why the other guy?"

"He didn't kill him, I did. Nico's best friend Ritchie was trying to cross him, but Nico didn't know it. Ritchie partnered up with this guy named Butch. Butch had beef with my ex-boyfriend Azar and put a gun to my head, threatening to kill me if I didn't give him Azar's money and the room key to where he was hiding out at. I didn't have a choice but to do what he asked and he murdered Azar.

"So the night Nico came looking for me at Ritchie's house, Butch showed up unexpectedly, and I killed him. Nobody knows that but you, Supreme. Nico probably has his suspicions, but he isn't sure. He also believes I took a million dollars from him, which I did. I wanted the money so I could leave Brooklyn and start my life over again."

"So where does pretty boy Mike fit in?"

"Mike is from Brooklyn. Before he got in the music game, he was a drug kingpin like Nico. When he met me at the club and I told him my name and that I was from Brooklyn he did some checking and realized that me and Nico's Precious was one in the same. When I ran into him at the studio he was delivering me a message courteous of Nico."

"What message was that?"

"Basically, that I still belong to him and when he gets out, he is going to kill me."

"Didn't he get two consecutive life sentences?"

"Yeah, but somehow, someway, he is determined to get out and get revenge."

"Baby, he's not ever getting out," Supreme said as he wiped away the tears that were streaming down my face.

"I know, but Mike sounded so sure that death was knocking on my front door. Supreme, I know I've done some fucked up things, but I'm different now. Falling in love with you has changed my whole outlook on life.

"I never thought another world existed outside of Brooklyn that I wanted to be a part of, but I was wrong. I know I've lied to you and you have every reason to turn your back on me, but just know that you're the first man I've ever loved, and I want you to be the last."

Supreme sat in front of me quiet as hell. I knew there were so many other secrets I was leaving out, but I didn't want to overload him. I just wanted to paint a clear picture of who I used to be. Plus, no matter what, some secrets have to die with you. I mean I had changed, but the streets of Brooklyn would always be in my blood.

"Precious, I'm glad you were honest with me. It explains why it was so hard for you to let down your guards. When I look in your beautiful eyes I can't believe you've been through so much. Most people carry the weight of the world on their face, yet you look as innocent as a little girl.

"All I want to do is take care of you and save you from yourself and the people who brought you so much pain. I could never turn my back on you. What you just told me only makes me love you more because I know how much courage it took for you to do that."

Supreme stood and came towards me. I was about to stand up, too, so I could embrace him for understanding and not judging me. "No sit back down." Supreme put his hand in his pocket and pulled out a tiny black box. Before what I thought he was about to do sunk in, he got on bended knee and said, "Precious, you're the only woman for me. I want to spend eternity with you. Would you do me the honor of becoming my wife?"

Remember when I said I came from nothing but was determined to have it all? That meant designer clothes, fly ass car, some diamonds and furs. You know the material things that all project chicks want. See, that was my hood dream.

When I rep'd for Brooklyn I had all that. Niggas couldn't tell me it could get no better. Every bitch in the street wanted to be me. I was Nico Carter's girl. We were the King and Queen of the hood. All motherfuckers had to bow down. I had my Alpo, so having it all had been accomplished in my book.

But now, here I was chilling on a beach that I arrived at on a yacht and before that a private jet, and Supreme, one of the biggest Rappers in the world, who I was madly in love with asked me to be his wife. So I'll admit it. I was wrong.

There is more to life than being 'Hood Rich'.

"Of course I'll marry you, Supreme. I love you more than anything in this world." After we danced under the moonlight and everyone left, Supreme and I made love on the beach. My life was finally at peace.

When Supreme and I got back from Barbados, I started planning our wedding immediately. The manner in which he proposed to me was so romantic that I wanted our wedding to be on the beach, too. I preferred a small ceremony, but Supreme wanted something extravagant. We compromised and decided to meet someplace in the middle.

I didn't have anyone to invite but Rhonda so the guest list would be comprised of all of his family and friends.

A week after we got back from our trip, Supreme took me to meet his mother and father, who also lived in Jersey. Supreme was originally from Queens, but once he made it big he bought his parents a big house in the suburbs. They were the sweetest couple and embraced me as if I was their own daughter.

Their only reservation was that Supreme and I were both so young, but they said as long as their son is happy then that's all that mattered. And it was obvious how happy Supreme and I were together.

*****

"I cant' believe you're moving out, Precious. I know you can't be married and living here with me, but couldn't you wait until after the wedding."

"Rhonda, I'ma miss you too, but my fiancée wants me to be with him. I love saying that."

"I bet you do. You're marrying Supreme. You're a lucky bitch."

"Who you telling? I can't wait for one of those groupie bitches to step to my man so I can flash my rock in they face and be like what?"

"You know in *Vibe Magazine,* they congratulated him on his engagement and they printed your name too."

"Word. I can' believe that."

"Yes, they also mentioned it on Miss Jones' show and Wendy Williams. So there are a lot of hurt bitches out there right now."

"Good, 'cause I ain't neva giving him up."

"Speaking of giving up, I know that wasn't Amir you were on the phone with a minute ago?"

"If I tell you 'yeah', will you hate me?"

"No, I'm not gonna hate you, but I will tell you to wise up."

"Precious, he's been trying so hard and he said he would go get counseling for his temper."

"Rhonda, listen if you not ready to settle down and be true to Amir all the counseling in the world ain't gonna help. He was dead-ass wrong for busting yo' ass, but in the same token, I knew that sneaky shit, fucking niggas behind his back, was gonna catch up to you.

"Trust me, Rhonda, I know what kind of damage cheating can cause. It can make the sanest motherfucker lose they mind. Niggas die behind shit like that.

"If you still want to run these streets and fuck this nigga and the third, then you need to be single and let Amir go. You shouldn't use him as a crutch, just in case it don't work out between you and one of the other dudes you messing around wit."

"I know you're right. It's difficult because before you came along and gave me a makeover, I was the corny chick that didn't nobody pay attention to. When guys started checking for me, it blew my mind. I do love Amir, but I feel like I have to make up for lost time."

"Girl, you can't neva make up for lost time. Once it's gone, it's gone. Only you can decide if you want to be with Amir or not, but if you're kicking him to the curb because you want to get your back blown out by some grimy-ass niggas, then you gotta check yourself. Because all them dudes want to do is smash and dash. Is that worth you losing somebody that you truly love? Don't answer that now, just think about it."

I went back in my room to pack up the rest of my belongings. I was going to miss this apartment and living with Rhonda. We really did become friends, and I had a lot of love for her. But it was time to close this chapter of my life. I was about to move on to something even better.

I picked up the only picture I had of my mother and stared into her beautiful green eyes. It was as if they were staring back at me. The picture was of her holding me when I was just a baby. Her face glowed and she appeared to be full of happiness. I can never remember a time growing up when my mother was healthy and drug-free, so I always hold on to this picture because this is the only tangible reminder I have that shows that she was. My mother still had so much to live for. Her life was stolen from her when she was only thirty-seven, and now here I was, twenty, about to walk down the aisle. It didn't seem fair.

Sometimes I stare at the picture for hours, looking for clues as to what went wrong. How did a woman that had the capabilities of having it all, live her life as though she was nothing? I wondered if she was looking down on me and knew how happy I was. Oh, how I wished she could be here to enjoy this with me. Planning my wedding, meeting my future husband and being a grandmother to the child I hoped to have in the future.

But most of all, I prayed that my mother had forgiven me. Right when she turned her life around, it was taken away because of the decisions I made. Hopefully turning my life around would be payment in full..

*****

It seemed like overnight it was the day of my wedding. With all the planning I did to have the event take place on a beach, we ended up having an elaborate ceremony right in our own backyard. With the growing guest list and celebratory parties people threw for us, it didn't make sense to try and fly everyone out to a beach. Plus, the mansion we lived on was sitting on six acres of land. That was more than enough space to have a lavish affair. Everyone from Michael Jordan to 50 Cent was in attendance.

It was the event of the summer. It took months to plan the wedding, but the actual ceremony lasted no more than fifteen minutes. But it was all worth it just to be at the altar with Supreme.

After we exchanged vows, took pictures and had our first dance as husband and wife, I went upstairs to change out of my wedding dress. Although it was beautiful I couldn't wait to step into the sexy Roberto Cavalli dress Supreme picked out for me. I caught every angle in the three-sided mirror and the dress clinched my body just right.

"You really are the most beautiful bride I've ever seen." I damn near tripped and fell when I turned to see who was intruding in my space.

"How did you get in here? You weren't even invited to the wedding."

"That was an oversight, I'm invited to everything." I wanted to smack the smug look off pretty boy Mike's face.

"That was no oversight. What the hell do you want anyway, to deliver another message?" I said sarcastically turning my back on him.

"As a matter of fact, yes. Nico said congratulations on your marriage."

"Oh really? so you told him I got married?"

"Actually he read about it in one of those magazines and when I spoke to him he asked me was it true. You know he still loves you, Precious, but how couldn't he look at you. You're about the closest thing you can get to perfection."

"GET OUT!"

"Calm down. You shouldn't get so upset on your wedding day."

"Then leave."

"I will, but only if you allow me to kiss you goodbye, on the cheek of course."

My body was motionless as my feet remained cemented to the floor. Mike came closer and I thought to myself, *the quicker he get his rocks off by giving me some weak-ass kiss, the quicker I'll be rid of him for good.* I held my breath as he put his head down to kiss me on the left side of my cheek. When I exhaled, he whispered in my ear, "Till death do you part."

Mike turned and vanished as quickly as he appeared. I didn't know whether to run after him and knock him in the head with my heel or to fall on the floor and burst out crying. This was my wedding day for heaven sakes, wasn't it everyone's obligation to stick to the script.

Dead or Alive

You know they say every time a child is born someone has to die. I pondered what man would sacrifice their existence in order to breathe life into my child. A month after Supreme and I got back from our honeymoon, I discovered we were pregnant. That's how he liked to think of it. I would remind him, though, that while we were pregnant, I was the one waking up every day with morning sickness.

I'd never seen Supreme happier than on the day I told him I was with child. Sometimes life can be too perfect.

"Good morning, my little man," Supreme said as he rubbed and kissed my stomach. That was his daily routine ever since he found out I was pregnant.

"Little man? How you know it's not my little princess?"

"My gut is telling me them back shots I gave you produced my little man, that's all."

"Them back shots? How 'bout when I was riding you like a cowgirl I made my little girl?"

"Yeah, but I only bust up in you from the back or the front, never with you on top."

"You do have a point there," I admitted clobbering him

over the head with the pillow.

"It don't matter, though, whether my little man or your little princess, it's nothing but love. I'm just ecstatic about my wife giving me my first seed."

"Baby, I'ma try so hard to be a good mother to our child. I wanna give this baby the type of parents I never had growing up."

"Precious, you're going to be a wonderful mother, and we will be great parents. This child's life is already starting off different than yours and mine."

"Supreme, you have great parents."

"Yeah, but I have the same hood story as mostly every other black man out here. I was blessed enough to grow up with both of my parents, but they had to break their backs to provide for us. We barely got by, and I could've easily turned my soul over to the street life, but this music game was my savior. Now I can provide for my people, and my family and kids won't ever have to struggle the way we did." Supreme sat up and put his arms around me as we lay in the bed.

"Precious, that's why when you made your confession to me, I didn't judge you or think any less of you. I know what desperation can make you do. Most people fold and either get strung out on drugs, commit suicide or lose they mind. Then they might as well be dead because they just floating through life anyway with no purpose. But your desperation gave you determination, and I admire you for that."

"With all I've seen and been through in life, I ain't never been one to have a lot of faith in God. But now I believe that prayers can be answered because only God could've brought someone as wonderful as you to me."

That morning Supreme and I began making love with a newfound intensity. With every thrust our bodies engulfed one another as if holding on for dear life. It was as if we were making love for the very last time.

After Supreme left to go to the studio in the city, I was looking at my day planner because his birthday was coming up and I wanted to surprise him with a party. When I stared at today's date, to my surprise I realized that it was the anniversary of my mother's murder. I had been so caught up in my new life that it slipped my mind. I got dressed and first stopped at Michael George in the city to pick up a flower arrangement to leave on her gravesite.

I dreaded going to Brooklyn, but I had to show my respect for my mother. I purposely wore a baseball cap and a black sweat suit in an attempt to disguise myself. I didn't feel there would be no drama, but you could never be too careful. Right as I turned on the Brooklyn Bridge, I heard my cell phone ringing.

It was Rhonda. "What's up?"

"Precious, can you come by? I really need someone to talk to."

"What's wrong?"

"It's Amir."

"Please don't tell me that nigga went upside yo' head again."

"No, but I'm afraid he's about to snap again. It's all my fault."

"What the fuck did you do Rhonda?"

"Not take your advice. Amir and I got back together, but I was still seeing other guys on the side. Somehow he got a hold of my T-mobile Sidekick messages and he read all the graphic shit I said I was going to do to this guy. Girl, he just called me and he is flipping out. I don't want to be alone, Precious."

"Okay I have to make a stop, but after I'm done, I'll come over. Lock the doors and don't let nobody in. If Amir come over there wigging out, call the police on his ass. I'll be there as soon as possible."

"Thank you so much, Precious."

"No problem, that's what friends are for."

When I pulled up to the cemetery I sat in the car for a minute seeing if I observed anyone or anything suspicious. I saw a few other families visiting gravesites but nothing out of the ordinary. When the coast seemed clear, I walked to my mother's burial site.

Ms. Duncan picked out a beautiful tombstone, and she had it engraved with exactly what I wanted it to say: *A Fallen Angel Who Is Now Forever At Peace*. I laid the flower arrangement down and while praying, I felt somebody walking up behind me. I was afraid to look to see who it was.

"Precious, is that you?" I heard a soft spoken woman say. I tilted my head to the side to get a glimpse of who was calling my name. I observed the familiar looking older woman.

"Ms. Duncan, how are you?" I stood up and gave her a hug.

"I thought that was you, Precious. It's so good to see you."

"It's good to see you, too."

"I was hoping I would see you here today. I've been try-ing to get in touch with you, but the cell number you gave me was out of service. And the only friend I knew you had was that girl Inga. But when I called, her mama told me that the poor child had been murdered."

"I heard about that. I'm sorry I never called you. I got a new phone and I never got around to giving you the number. Is everything OK, do you need some money or something? I'd be more than happy to help you out. Especially since you gave my mother such a beautiful funeral."

"Oh, no, honey. I don't need your money. I still have plenty left over from what you gave me the first time. This is about you, Precious."

"Me? What about me?"

"Precious, I wanted to warn you."

"Warn me about what?"

"You know I got a son, Darius, he's a few years older than you. But like so many of our young black boys, he got caught up in them streets.

"He got out of jail a few months ago, and he's been back at home, staying with me. Well, a few days ago, him and some of his friends were running their mouths like they always do, but when I heard them mention your name, I started paying close attention. They said a fellow by the name of Nico Carter was getting out of jail soon and the first person he was coming to see was you."

"You must've misunderstood. Nico is doing life in prison. That's a mistake."

"No, Precious. They said some big time lawyer he has was able to get him out on some sort of technicality."

My whole body became weak as I stood denying over and over again that Ms. Duncan was mistaken. "Precious, baby, are you going to be alright? Why don't we go over there and have a seat on one of those benches."

"I can't. I have to go … to go, Ms. Duncan," I said stuttering every word.

"Precious, wait," Ms. Duncan yelled out to me, but it was too late. I got in my car and drove off so fast, trying my best to run away from the truth. I took off my baseball cap and freed my hair, hoping it would stop the migraine headache I was now suffering. I was trying to think who I could call to see if Ms. Duncan's information was correct.

She said he would be getting out soon that meant he was still locked up and I had time to get to the bottom of everything. I thought about getting a hold of pretty boy Mike, but I had sworn to Supreme that I would never speak to him again. *Maybe Rhonda could speak to Mike for me and see if he had any information about Nico's release,* I thought.

I have to go see her anyway. After I help her come up with a solution regarding Amir, then I'll ask her to help me out with Mike.

When I pulled up to my old apartment building my stomach felt queasy, and it wasn't morning sickness. The moment I got to Rhonda's front door and saw it slightly open, I knew something was terribly wrong.

"Rhonda," I called out, and got no response. Everything seemed in order and, for a brief second, I thought maybe Rhonda ran out and forgot to lock the door. That thought was put to rest when I opened her bedroom door and she was spread out eagle style with her wrist and ankles tied up to each bedpost. Her naked body was bruised and beaten. There was a pillow over her face, and I removed it, only to find duct tape covering her mouth and her face was blown off. This was almost like reliving finding my mother all over again.

"That sonofabitch Amir. I can't believe he did this to you, Rhonda. I told you not to let him in," I screamed out loud as if she could really hear me. I picked up my cell phone and dialed 911. "Yes there has been a murder at 100 Crown Court, Edgewater, New Jersey. Her boyfriend Amir Jacobs is the killer."

I sat on the couch waiting for the police to show up. The wait wasn't long; within five minutes they were at the door. "Miss, are you the one who called about a murder?"

"Yes, I am."

"Where's the crime scene?"

"The bedroom on your left," I said pointing them in the direction of Rhonda's room.

"I know that you're upset but can you please answer a few questions for my partner here?"

"No problem." The police detective pulled out a notepad.

"Miss, what is your name?"

"Precious Cummings. I'm sorry, Precious Mills I recently got married."

Congratulations."

"Thanks," I said awkwardly.

"How do you know the deceased?"

"We were roommates until I moved in with my husband."

"So if you no longer live here what made you come by?"

"We were still friends." The officer nodded his head. I knew he wanted me to get to the point, but my mind was cluttered, thinking about Rhonda's death and Nico's impending release. "She called me today and asked me to come over. She was having problems with her boyfriend, and she was scared he was going to hurt her."

"She told you that?"

"Yes."

"Those were her words that she believed he was going to hurt her?"

"Yes. They had broken up before because he caught her cheating on him and he beat the shit out of her. I'm sorry excuse my language."

"What's her boyfriend's name?"

"Amir Jacobs."

"OK, go right ahead Mrs. Mills."

"He knocked her up pretty good and only stopped because I walked in on him and threatened to call the police. *They didn't need to know he stopped because I pulled out a 9mm on his ass* I thought to myself. "They recently got back together, and he started checking her Sidekick messages and found out that she was cheating again. She was petrified that he was going to flip out on her again, and she asked me to come be with her. If only I had gotten here sooner."

"Don't blame yourself, Mrs. Mills. When you're dealing with scum bags like this, there is nothing you can do. You're lucky you weren't here. Then I might be investigating two homicides. Excuse me I'm going to have a warrant issued for Mr. Jacobs' arrest."

I sat on the couch for thirty minutes, unable to move until the paramedics brought out Rhonda's body, and I stood up, reaching towards her, wanting to believe she wasn't dead.

"Mrs. Mills the New York City Police Department has Amir Jacobs in custody, and I'm on my way to the city to question him."

"They found him in New York? He wasn't hiding out?"

"Actually, Mrs. Mills he was at work when they picked

him up. When we ran his name, we called the number he was listed under and a woman answered the phone. She identified herself as his wife and said her husband was at work. We called his job and they confirmed that, but they still brought him in for questioning because you can never be too sure."

"Married? Amir was married?"

"That's what the lady said. You know how men can be sometimes. They have their own secrets."

"So what are you saying, Amir didn't kill Rhonda?"

"I can't give you a definite answer on that. If his story checks out, and he was at work as his boss has confirmed, then, no, Mr. Jacobs is not the one who is responsible for your friend's death. I have your number and will call to keep you updated. But here's my card, just in case you have any questions."

I left Rhonda's apartment more confused than ever. I didn't know what was going on. If Amir didn't kill her, then who? She was seeing a few different dudes, but which one of them would want to see her dead? Whoever did that to Rhonda wanted to torture her. The person was enraged. I couldn't imagine Rhonda having any enemies like that. I had to speak to Supreme. His phone was just ringing and he finally picked it up right when I was about to hang up. "Baby, I'm so glad you answered your phone."

"Precious, what's wrong?"

"Everything. Rhonda's been murdered."

"What!"

"Baby, yes. She asked me to stop by, and when I got there, she was tied to her bed with her face blown off. Somebody murdered her."

"Do they know who did it?"

"At first I thought it was Amir, but he might have an airtight alibi. This shit is freaking me out, Supreme."

"Precious, calm down. You're pregnant. You can't let yourself get all upset."

"Baby, please come home. There is something else I want to talk to you about, too."

"OK, I'm leaving the studio right now."

"I love you, Supreme."

"I love you, too."

Death seemed to follow me. I knew Rhonda's murder had nothing to do with me, but I felt like I was right in the center of it. I thought I had left all the bloodshed in Brooklyn but now it was here in Jersey. The gate leading up to the driveway opened, and I turned my head to look because I felt as if someone was behind me. There was nothing there. I put my head down and said, "Precious, relax. You need to stay calm for the baby."

I put my hand on my stomach, "Everything will be alright, my little angel. Your daddy will make sure of that."

Once I talked to Supreme about the conversation I had with Ms. Duncan, I wouldn't feel so stressed. Supreme was good at coming up with solutions. Maybe he could pay Nico off, or if necessary, have him killed. However it went, Supreme would work it out. Or so I thought. My whole life seemed to move in slow motion after stepping out my car. There stood the ghost from my past. Only it wasn't a ghost.

"You've done very well for yourself. I'm proud of you, Precious."

I closed my eyes because I knew this wasn't real. It was like those nightmares that made it impossible for me to sleep for days. But just like when I would wake up, that image standing before me would be gone.

"Baby, open your eyes I'm not going anywhere. I'm the real deal."

"Nico, you can't be real."

"Precious, you're just as beautiful, if not more, than the first time I saw you walking the streets of Harlem. I knew you didn't belong there. Now look at you, married to a superstar, living in a mansion.

"You made Brooklyn proud. But as much as you cleaned yourself up, you still have those dark eyes just like me. Remember I told you besides me and my father you were the only other person I ever met with the same darkness in your eyes. That right there should've been enough incentive for me to let you walk away that day, but instead I wanted you more. Because of that I had to pay the price for my decision. Now it's time for you to pay the price for yours."

"Nico, please, I was so immature back then and I made a mistake. But I'm a different person now. I've put the streets behind me and turned my life around."

"It's all good that you turned your life around, but you had to give my soul to the devil in order to get it. Not once did you think about the life you took away from me, and the money you stole. You destroyed everything we had over some pussy. A bitch I didn't even give a fuck about.

"But that didn't matter to you, because you're like me. Your pride and your ego dictate your moves. But, Precious, with every decision you make in life, there are consequences. And your consequence is death."

"Nico, don't. What can I do to stop this? I don't want to

die."

"You're already dead I just came to take it in blood. But because I still have mad love for you, Precious, I won't make you suffer the way I did your friend."

"What friend?" At first I thought he was speaking of Ritchie, but he knew I did that for revenge so what friend could he be talking about?

"If I'm not mistaken her name was Rhonda," he said with that same devious chuckle I always detested.

"You killed Rhonda, but why?"

"I really didn't want to take the chance and come here to kill you. I wasn't sure what type of security you were working with, but obviously not enough," he said, glancing around the estate. You know Mike. Well he told me about your ex-roommate Rhonda. So I paid her an unexpected visit.

"All I asked her to do was get you over to the apartment, and I would handle the rest, but she refused. I figured if I tortured her a little bit she would give in, but she was a fighter. She was a true friend to the end unlike Inga."

I can't believe Rhonda died trying to save my life. She knew I was coming to see her anyway, all she had to do was tell Nico to wait. Rhonda sacrificed her life for me, damn.

"Nico, hasn't there been enough death in our lives? I can give you back the million dollars and more, if you like. I have a husband, Nico and I'm pregnant with his child. I'm living the life I never dreamed possible. Don't take that away from me."

"I came back for you to take what's mine, and that's your life." Nico raised his gun, and we both turned when we heard Supreme's driver pulling up. As his car got closer,

Supreme could see that Nico was pointing his gun at me. He jumped out and his bodyguards followed with guns raised.

But it was too late. The loud explosion ripped through my chest. The pressure jolted me back, and I hit my car before falling down to the ground. Then I heard Nico shooting in the direction of Supreme and his bodyguards as he vanished in the darkness. Supreme ran to me cradling my limp body.

"Precious, baby, it's me, Supreme. Please stay with me. The ambulance will be here any minute. Baby, please just hold on."

"Supreme, I'm so happy I was able to see your face one last time. Baby, I love you. I never knew what love was until I found you. Please forgive me for leaving you and taking our baby too."

Supreme held me so tightly and I gathered all the strength from within, trying to keep my eyes open because the sight of Supreme's face was giving me the will to live. But as my blood continued to flow, my strength deteriorated and my body wanted to be at peace. The last words I heard before my eyelids shut was Supreme's begging God not to let me die.

A KING PRODUCTION

Dior Comes Home...

Rich
or
Famous
Part 2

JOY DEJA KING

Prologue

Lorenzo stepped out of his black Bugatti Coupe and entered the non-descript building in East Harlem. Normally, Lorenzo would have at least one henchman with him, but he wanted complete anonymity. When he made his entrance, the man Lorenzo planned on hiring was patiently waiting.

"I hope you came prepared for what I need."

"I wouldn't have wasted my time if I hadn't," Lorenzo stated before pulling out two pictures from a manila envelope and tossing them on the table.

"This is her?"

"Yes, her name is Alexus. Study this face very carefully, 'cause this is the woman you're going to bring to me, so I can kill."

"Are you sure you don't want me to handle it? Murder is included in my fee."

"I know, but personally killing this backstabbing snake is a gift to myself"

"Who is the other woman?"

"Her name is Lala."

"Do you want her dead, too?"

"I haven't decided. For now, just find her whereabouts and any other pertinent information. She also has a young daughter. I want you to find out how the little girl is doing. That will determine whether Lala lives or dies."

"Is there anybody else on your hit list?"

"This is it for now, but that might change at any moment. Now, get on your job, because I want results ASAP," Lorenzo demanded before tossing stacks of money next to the photos.

"I don't think there's a need to count. I'm sure it's all there," the hit man said, picking up one of the stacks and flipping through the bills.

"No doubt, and you can make even more, depending on how quickly I see results."

"I appreciate the extra incentive."

"It's not for you, it's for me. Everyone that is responsible for me losing the love of my life will pay in blood. The sooner the better."

Lorenzo didn't say another word and instead made his exit. He came and delivered; the rest was up to the hit man he had hired. But Lorenzo wasn't worried, he was just one of the many killers on his payroll hired to do the exact same job. He wanted to guarantee that Alexus was delivered to him alive. In his heart, he not only blamed Alexus and Lala for getting him locked up, but also held both of them responsible for Dior taking her own life. As he sat in his jail cell, Lorenzo promised himself that once he got out, if need be he would spend the rest of his life making sure both women received the ultimate retribution.

A KING PRODUCTION

Power

NO ONE MAN SHOULD HAVE ALL THAT POWER...BUT THERE WERE TWO

JOY DEJA KING

Chapter 1

Underground King

Alex stepped into his attorney's office to discuss what was always his number one priority…business. When he sat down their eyes locked and there was complete silence for the first few seconds. This was Alex's way of setting the tone of the meeting. His silence spoke volumes. This might've been his attorney's office but he was the head nigga in charge and nothing got started until he decided it was time to speak. Alex felt this approach was necessary. You see, after all these years of them doing business, attorney George Lofton still wasn't used to dealing with a man like Alex; a dirt-poor kid who could've easily died in the projects he was born in, but instead made millions. It wasn't done the ski mask way but it was still illegal.

They'd first met when Alex was a sixteen-year-old kid growing up in TechWood Homes, a housing project in Atlanta. Alex and his best friend, Deion, had been arrested because the principal found 32 crack vials in

Alex's book bag. Another kid had tipped the principal off and the principal subsequently called the police. Alex and Deion were arrested and suspended from school. His mother called George, who had the charges against them dismissed and they were allowed to go back to school. But that wasn't the last time he would use George. He was arrested at twenty-two for attempted murder and for trafficking cocaine a year later. Alex was acquitted on both charges. George Lofton later became known as the best trial attorney in Atlanta, but Alex had also become the best at what he did. And since it was Alex's money that kept Mr. Lofton in designer suits, million dollar homes and foreign cars, he believed he called the shots, and dared his attorney to tell him differently.

Alex noticed that what seemed like a long period of silence made Mr. Lofton feel uncomfortable, which he liked. Out of habit, in order to camouflage the discomfort, his attorney always kept bottled water within arm's reach. He would cough then take a swig, lean back in his chair, raise his eyebrows a little, trying to give a look of certainty, though he wasn't completely confident at all in Alex's presence. The reason was because Alex did what many had thought would be impossible, especially men like George Lofton. He had gone from a knucklehead, low-level drug dealer to an underground king and an unstoppable respected criminal boss.

Before finally speaking, Alex gave an intense stare into George Lofton's piercing eyes. They were not only the bluest he had ever seen, but also some of the most calculating. The latter is what Alex found so compelling. A calculating attorney working on his behalf could almost guarantee a get out of jail card for the duration of his criminal career.

"Have you thought over what we briefly discussed the other day?" Alex asked his attorney, finally breaking the silence.

"Yes I have, but I want to make sure I understand you correctly. You want to give me six hundred thousand to represent you or your friend Deion if you are ever arrested and have to stand trial again in the future?"

Alex assumed he had already made himself clear based on their previous conversations and was annoyed by what he now considered a repetitive question. "George, you know I don't like repeating myself. That's exactly what I'm saying. Are we clear?"

"So this is an unofficial retainer."

"Yes, you can call it that."

George stood and closed the blinds then walked over to the door that led to the reception area. He turned the deadbolt so they wouldn't be disturbed. George sat back behind the desk. "You know that if you and your friend Deion are ever on the same case that I can't represent the both of you."

"I know that."

"So what do you propose I do if that was ever to happen?"

"You would get him the next best attorney in Atlanta," Alex said without hesitation. Deion was Alex's best friend—had been since the first grade. They were now business partners, but the core of their bond was built on that friendship, and because of that Alex would always look out for Deion's best interest.

"That's all I need to know."

Alex clasped his hands and stared at the ceiling for a moment thinking that maybe it was a bad idea bringing the money to George. Maybe he should have just put it somewhere safe only known to him and his mom. He quickly dismissed his concerns.

"Okay. Where's the money?" Alex presented him with two leather briefcases. George opened the first one and was glad to see that it was all hundred-dollar bills. When he closed the briefcase he asked, "There is no need to count this is there?"

"You can count it if you want, but it's all there."

George took another swig of water. The cash made him nervous. He planned to take it directly to one of his bank safe deposit boxes. The two men stood. Alex was a foot taller than George; he had flawless mahogany skin, a deep brown with a bit of a red tint, broad shoulders, very large hands, and a goatee. He was a man's man. With such a powerful physical appearance, Alex kept his style very low-key. His only display of wealth was a pricey diamond watch that his best friend and partner Deion had bought him for his birthday.

"I'll take good care of this, and you," his attorney said, extending his hand to Alex.

"With this type of money, I know you will," Alex

stated without flinching. Alex gave one last lingering stare into his attorney's piercing eyes. "We do have a clear understanding…correct?"

"Of course. I've never let you down and I never will. That, I promise you." The men shook hands and Alex made his exit with the same coolness as his entrance.

With Alex embarking on a new, potentially dangerous business venture, he wanted to make sure that he had all his bases covered. The higher up he seemed to go on the totem pole, the costlier his problems became. But Alex welcomed new challenges because he had no intentions of ever being a nickel and dime nigga again.

A King A King Production
Order Form

A King Production
P.O. Box 912
Collierville, TN 38027
www.joydejaking.com
www.twitter.com/joydejaking

Name: _____

Address: _____

City/State: _____

Zip: _____

QUANTITY	TITLES	PRICE	TOTAL
_____	Bitch	$15.00	_____
_____	Bitch Reloaded	$15.00	_____
_____	The Bitch Is Back	$15.00	_____
_____	Queen Bitch	$15.00	_____
_____	Last Bitch Standing	$15.00	_____
_____	Superstar	$15.00	_____
_____	Ride Wit' Me	$12.00	_____
_____	Stackin' Paper	$15.00	_____
_____	Trife Life To Lavish	$15.00	_____
_____	Trife Life To Lavish II	$15.00	_____
_____	Stackin' Paper II	$15.00	_____
_____	Rich or Famous	$15.00	_____
_____	Bitch A New Beginning	$15.00	_____
_____	Mafia Princess Part 1	$15.00	_____
_____	Mafia Princess Part 2	$15.00	_____
_____	Mafia Princess Part 3	$15.00	_____
_____	Mafia Princess Part 4	$15.00	_____
_____	Boss Bitch	$15.00	_____
_____	Baller Bitches Vol. 1	$15.00	_____
_____	Baller Bitches Vol. 2	$15.00	_____
_____	Bad Bitch	$15.00	_____
_____	Princess Fever "Birthday Bash"	$9.99	_____

Shipping/Handling (Via Priority Mail) $6.50 1-2 Books, $8.95 3-4 Books add $1.95 for ea. Additional book.

Total: $_____ **FORMS OF ACCEPTED PAYMENTS:** Certified or government issued checks and money Orders, all mail in orders take 5-7 Business days to be delivered.